THE
WALK-IN

By

Sandy Harrington

This book is dedicated to

My daughters, Lee and CG

And

My grandson, Christian Blake Reilly

TABLE OF CONTENTS

Chapter 1

Jason

Streaks of lightning expose the high elevation of western North Carolina. As ominous clouds gather over the Brushy Mountains, thudding hooves and breaking twigs echo in the dark woods as a frightened deer scrambles for shelter. Startled by shadowy lights, the buck stops, tilts his head and listens. Hearing sounds of laughter, the white-tailed animal freezes in its tracks.

The wooden legs of the canvas stool sink deeper into the red clay as Deacon John shifts his weight and exclaims, "Okay, this is the tie breaker. What three men did King Nebuchadnezzar throw into the fiery furnace?"

I holler, "Shadrack, Meshak and Abednego!"

Knowing full well I'm not a regular churchgoer, Jimmy is stunned by my correct answer and challenges, "How in the world did you know that?"

Excited, I jump up and claim victory. Bowing

before my audience of five, I look down at Jimmy and report, "My grandma told me that story when I was little. I never forget the names 'cause the first two rhyme and the last one sounds like 'to bed we go.'"

I take off my yellow, fur-lined nylon jacket, squat down and roll it up into a ball. Using it as a pillow, I lie down on the hard ground. Deacon John leans over and tosses a log on the dwindling fire. As the flames crackle and hiss, burning embers spew skyward. I focus on one spark as it floats heavenly bound.

Seeing dark clouds robbing the moon of its light, I hear my dad's words in my head, *"Bad weather is forecast. It's gonna rain like cats and dogs. Do you really want to be cold and wet in the woods when you could be warm and dry at home?"*

As the deacon drones on about religion, I think, *Dad has changed since we moved to Asheville. He is overprotective. He thinks Deacon John is a 'goody-two shoes' and not manly enough to chaperone boys in the woods . He insisted I bring his old pocketknife, compass and miniature flashlight in case I got lost. ... Mom hasn't changed a bit since we moved here. She encourages me to make new friends and try different things. Dad may wear the pants in the family; but she holds the belt.*

Hearing laughter, I snap back to reality. I look at Jimmy and smile. He could be a model for a Normal Rockwell painting. He is the typical, mischievous redhead. His big brown eyes, countless freckles and constant jabbering have earned him the reputation of 'class clown.'

I glance over at Steve whose the biggest thirteen-year old I've ever met. Standing five feet six inches, he has icy blue eyes and a bad case of acne. Despite his tousled, mousy brown hair, wrinkled clothes and dirty fingernails, Steve is the most popular boy at school. Nobody challenges him in a contact sport, including myself.

Looking over at Charlie, I grin and acknowledge the youngest and smallest boy in the group. He is only eleven and has a clear complexion. Charlie's green eyes reflect a jealous glint. His shoulder-length blonde hair looks silly with color-coordinated, stiffly pressed clothes. Oftentimes, I tease Charlie by calling him a 'neat freak.'

I turn my head to stare at the most distant youngster at camp. Rusty is a tall boy for twelve with a scrawny physique. His dark hair and eyes project a sad, mysterious quality. Always clad in a tee shirt and jeans, Rusty makes a point of being aloof. It is painfully obvious he doesn't enjoy our company and would rather be anywhere in the world but here.

Deacon John raises his voice an octave to capture my attention. Pretending to listen, I concentrate on his physical characteristics. Balding, the deacon has more hair on his eyebrows than he does on his head. Beady brown eyes magnified by thick, horn-rimmed glasses and a wrinkled forehead disguise the fact he is only thirty-four. And the fifty extra pounds he carries make him appear shorter than his actual height of six foot three inches.

Feeling the need to compare my appearance with the other guys, I have to admit I'm pretty good-looking. Thanks to good genes, I've got sky-blue eyes, pitch-black hair, cleft in my chin and olive complexion. My height and weight are average for my age; so, it's obvious I'm not an immediate threat to Steve. But, my walnut-sized biceps show potential.

Deacon John distracts my power of observation when he gets up and heads to the cabin. Before we boys have a chance to enjoy being out from under his watchful gaze, our chaperone comes back carrying wire sticks and marshmallows. He hands out the straightened clothes hangers and waits patiently while we dig in the bag for handfuls of soft, white spongy treats.

Glancing over at the antisocial boy sitting on a distant rock, Deacon John hollers for Rusty to join us. The loner stares into space and ignores the offer. Unaffected by his rejection, the deacon waves him off and turns his attention back to us as we roast marshmallows over the open fire.

As we gobble down the delicious treats, we guys swap stories. The deacon throws more logs on the fire and sits back down on his stool. He waits several minutes before clapping his hands to gain our undivided attention. Taking over the conversation, he begins preaching about the do's and don'ts of life. Bored out of my mind, I resume my earlier position and stretch out on the ground. Staring up at the dark clouds, I recall …

I was up and out of bed before Mom had a chance to wake me. I ran into the kitchen and raced for the fridge. Using the red pen attached to the calendar, I crossed off the date, Friday, August 21. Then, I sprinted over to the backdoor, opened it and took a deep gulp of air. As the grass glistened with dew, a cool breeze blew into the house. I thought, 'Dad's wrong. The weather is perfect for camping.'

After picking up Jimmy, we headed for the church. Too excited to sit still, me and Jimmy bounced around in the backseat of the family car, a brand-new 1987 Buick station wagon. Thinking he was driving way too slow, I leaned forward and asked, "Dad, can't you drive a little faster?"

Jimmy sprang forward and echoed, "Yeah, Mr. Frazier, put the pedal to the metal!"

Dad deliberately kept driving slower than a snail and looked at us through the rearview mirror. In a calm voice, he replied, "I'm not going to get a ticket racing to get you guys to the church on time."

His remark reminded Mom of an old song. She laughed as she sang, "I'm getting married in the morning. Ding, dong! the bells are gonna chime ... Hail and salute me. Then haul off and boot me ... And get me to the church, Get me to the church ... For Gawd's sake, get me to the church on time!"

Me and Jimmy giggled as she sang off key. Dad pretended to be annoyed and chided, "You're not nearly as funny as you think you are."

Mom quipped, "And, you're in no risk of getting a ticket. Cops don't give tickets to men who drive like little old ladies."

As he struggled not to laugh out loud, Jimmy spied a minivan parked in the church parking lot. He pointed as he shouted, "There they are! Pull over, Mr. Frazier!"

Dad pulled up to the curb. Deacon John motioned for me and Jimmy to come on. We hopped out of the car, grabbed our gear and raced to the church van. Glancing back at my parents, I saw Mom mouth the words, "I love you."

Deep, heavy rolling sounds of thunder send chills down my spine. I open my eyes and look around. Seeing that no one else is alarmed by the prospect of rain, I close my eyes and continue to daydream.

All of us boys gave our chaperone the third degree on the way to the campsite. As we sped up the two-lane highway, Deacon John elaborated, "We're going to a cabin in the woods where I used to hunt with my dad. It's a beautiful spot with green grass and tall trees. There's a creek full of large boulders, where we can wade in the water and fish for our supper. The location is so remote the only voices you'll hear are your own echoes."

After several hours of driving, Deacon John turned off the highway onto a gravel road. The van bumped and swayed as it ran over rocks and dropped into holes. Halfway up the mountain, a wooden gate blocked the road. Steve hopped out and opened it so we could get through. Then, the road became more of a path and our vehicle crawled along like an inchworm. About noon, the deacon pulled over and parked under a large pine tree.

Eager to get out of the vehicle, all of us boys jumped out and waited for orders. As he opened the rear of the van, Deacon John explained, "We have to hike about two miles." He took a deep breath and added, "Let's grab a snack before we go."

As the group retrieved their snacks, Jimmy and me ran for a large boulder and sat down. I emptied my pockets. Several articles fell out. Jimmy giggled as he picked up a notepad and pen. He remarked, "I get all that other stuff but what's this?"

Knowing there would be no peace until I answered his question, I explained, "I want to be a reporter when I grow up. I keep notes when I do something special."

Jimmy jumped up and grinned like a Cheshire cat. As he danced around me, he exclaimed, "Write a story about me! Make me a super hero!"

In a serious tone, I retorted, "Reporters don't make heroes. They report the facts."

Jimmy shook his finger at me and argued, "That ain't what my dad says. He says reporters twist the truth to sell papers."

Frustrated by his attitude, I shouted, "Geez Louise! If it will make you happy, I'll make you the hero!"

Jimmy laughed and ran in circles around me, chiding, "My dad is always right! You just proved it! You're willing to bend the truth to write your story!"

The two of us chased each other around trees. Our antics were interrupted when Deacon John clapped his hands for attention. We sprinted over and joined the rest of the group in time to be handed gear from the van. Everyone strapped on their backpacks and headed into the woods.

Speaking loud so everybody could hear him, Deacon John warned, "Watch out for branches, rocks and rabbit holes! Keep your eyes peeled for snakes and wild animals! Above all, don't wander off!" Then, he continued, "I'm responsible for your welfare! So, don't cause me any grief!"

Somewhat frightened by the words, 'snakes and wild animals,' we boys glanced around at each other and hustled to close the gap, staying on the deacon's heels. Suddenly, the hike had become a real-life adventure with the threat of danger lurking behind every tree. Walking in single file, the going got rough. The narrow path led up and down steep hills. In some areas, the underbrush was so thick we had to jump over plants, shrubs and broken tree limbs. A few times, one of us would stumble and fall 'cause we stepped in a hole or tripped over a rock. After a while, we all relaxed our guard. I used my compass to track our hike. I was beginning to feel like a real mountaineer and even got a little cocky. I saw a wood shed supported by cement blocks. I wanted to explore the dilapidated shack. I grabbed Jimmy's arm and pulled him toward the abandoned lean-to.

Deacon John spotted us veer off course and read my mind. He shouted, "Oh, no you don't! That building's gotta be rotten!

It could collapse on top of you! Get back in line and keep up the pace!"

Falling back into line, I winked at Jimmy and whispered, "Let's sneak back up here later and find out just how sturdy that old shack really is."

Jimmy rolled his eyes and giggled, "I knew you came along for a purpose. You're gonna get us lost. Then, the deacon will have to come and find us."

A loud rumble of thunder disturbs my thoughts. I open my eyes and see the deacon looking at me. I smile and nod my head in agreement to whatever he just said. Then, I notice Steve's eyes are shut and almost laugh out loud. I see Jimmy drawing in the dirt. I glance at Charlie and can't believe he is eating up every word the deacon spits out. I have no interest in what Rusty's doing so I don't even bother to check him out. Instead, I shut my eyes and continue recalling the day's activities.

About 'twoish,' we reached a small, rustic cabin overlooking a mountain stream. An open fire pit covered by a rusty, metal grill occupied a clearing about twenty feet away. Ashes and sticks were scattered all over the place, making it obvious other people had recently camped here.

Deacon John walked in a circle, stretched out his arms and shouted, "This is God's country!" He listened for his echo before continuing, "We're alone in the wild and must depend on each other for survival. Let's set up camp."

Our chaperone took out a key and unlocked the cabin door. We followed him inside. It was a one-room shack with only the barest of furnishings. An old, wooden table with six mismatched chairs sat in the center of the room and eight cots lined the walls. A cluster of cabinets hung over the corner fireplace which appeared to be out of commission 'cause no logs were anywhere in sight.

Everybody selected a cot and rolled out their sleeping bags. While we emptied our backpacks, Deacon John walked over to the cabinets and began pulling down supplies. He stacked canned food, bottled water, paper plates, plastic forks, napkins and an assortment of cookware on the table.

After putting the cabin in order, Deacon John picked up two fishing poles that were propped in a corner and headed outside. We followed him and waited for instructions. He stood over the open pit and said, "We need wood."

Eager to please him, all of us boys ran in different directions, searching for kindling. As we scattered, Deacon John hollered, "Not too far, boys! Remember there are snakes and wild animals around here!"

As soon as we got back with dry wood, Deacon John piled it on top of the open stove. After a few tries at igniting the kindling, the fire lit. It crackled and hissed as flames leapt high into the air.

Satisfied the fire wasn't going to die out, the deacon looked at his watch and said, "It's almost two thirty. Steve and Charlie take the fishing poles and head down to the stream. Jimmy and

Jason go with 'em. Rusty and I are going to scout the area and make certain no other campers are in the vicinity."

Deacon John winked at Rusty and motioned for him to lead the way. Although I was curious why those two were going on a scouting expedition alone, I didn't say anything. I simply nodded my head and followed the other boys down to the creek.

Steve and Charlie fished while me and Jimmy waded in the cold, mountain stream. We took turns standing on the large rocks and sliding into the water. Steve managed to catch three large fresh-water trout. The four of us forgot about time until we started getting hungry. When his stomach growled several times, Steve suggested we head back to camp.

Cold and wet from the icy cold water, me and Jimmy were trembling so hard our teeth chattered. Neither of us needed much persuasion. We were more than ready to get back to a warm, cozy fire. When we reached camp, Deacon John and Rusty weren't back yet. None of us were overly alarmed but we were concerned. Steve checked his watch and said, "It's nearly five o'clock. I can't imagine what's taking them so long. Surely, they haven't gotten lost."

Getting nervous, Charlie asked, "What if you're wrong and they are lost?"

Jimmy answered for me, saying, "Don't worry. Jason has a compass. If they don't come back, he can lead ..."

Before he could finish his sentence, we all heard a rustle in the woods. Our eyes opened real wide. We all held our breath, not knowing what to expect! Deacon John walked out of the woods first. Rusty followed close behind him. Our chaperone *appeared to be on a spiritual high. In a cheerful voice, he shouted, "I see our fellow campers have survived without us? I've worked up quite an appetite!" He rubbed his belly and questioned, Did you catch any fish?"*

Charlie held up the trout. Deacon John beamed with delight. He stacked more wood on the pit, fanned the hot embers and set the fire ablaze. Hissing, the flames danced in rhythm to the cool mountain breeze. The deacon took the fish out of Charlie's hand and placed their dead carcasses on a large rock. He took his hunting knife out of its sheath and rubbed it across his pants. Without hesitating, he chopped off the heads and tails, slit the skin from top to bottom and gutted the fish with the tip of his blade

Amazed and impressed at how skillfully the deacon manipulated his knife, I stood and watched for a few moments. Then, I remembered my manners and helped the other boys fix the rest of the meal. We all worked together, except Rusty. Looking flushed, he kept his head low. Grimacing, he sat down on a large boulder and refused to make eye contact with anybody. When we were ready to chow down, Steve called Rusty to join us. He ignored the invitation. Instead, he walked over to the rock where the deacon had cleaned the fish and sat down. With his back to Rusty, Deacon John smiled at us and said, "Just ignore him. He'll eat when he gets hungry."

I blink and open my eyes. My stomach is queasy from eating too many marshmallows. Hoping the nausea will pass, I sit up and join in the conversation. Much to my chagrin, Deacon John interrupts and begins sermonizing again. I roll my eyes at Jimmy, complain of a stomachache and lie back down. I stare at the blazing fire for a few moments before looking up at the threatening sky. Thinking, *this is the best day of my life*, I yawn, close my eyes and fall asleep.

Chapter 2

Terror

Hearing loud voices, I wake up and rub my eyes. The first thing I see is Rusty standing in front of the fire. Holding his hands behind his back, he rocks back and forth on his heels, glaring at the deacon. All of us boys look up and acknowledge him but our chaperone pays him no attention. Extremely agitated, Rusty expels his anger by screaming, " You perverted bastard! You sit here and preach religion, when you are the devil himself!"

Deacon John ignores Rusty's insult. The youngster stomps his foot in anger! Rage engulfs him and takes control of his actions! He screams and runs at the deacon! As he brandishes the hunting knife menacingly, the rest of us are startled as the firelight catches the glitter of the blade! We sit paralyzed on the ground and don't make a sound! The deacon has his back to Rusty and doesn't see the weapon! He makes no attempt to get out of the way! Running, Rusty screams, "You've put your filthy hands on me for the last time!"

The boy stabs the deacon in the shoulder! The big man screams in shock and pain! He jumps up and grabs for the knife! Rusty manages to slash his hand before being subdued! Deacon John jerks the knife out of his clutches! The youngster becomes hysterical, screaming and sobbing as he gasps, "I hate you! I hate you! I'm going to tell every member of the church what you've been doing to me!"

As blood dampens his shirt, Deacon John holds Rusty firmly in his grasp! Wincing in pain, he turns to look at us and shakes his head! We stand spellbound, caught in the surreal moment! None of us moves or speaks, hoping if we don't acknowledge the assault it will vanish like a ghost in the night! The deacon exclaims, "I have no idea what Rusty is talking about! He has lost his ever loving mind!" He continues to hold tight to the boy, speaking in gasps, "I've given this boy the same spiritual guidance as the rest of you! I've tried to teach him right from wrong but what can you expect from a child who crawled out of Shantytown?"

Rusty becomes rabid with rage! He looks from Jimmy to Steve as he fights for the truth, screaming, "Bull shit! Has he screwed you, Jimmy? What about you, Steve? Has he forced you to suck his cock?" Jimmy and Steve shake their heads, while Charlie and me remain transfixed! Rusty continues to fight for the truth, yelling, "Yeah, that's what I thought! The good deacon prefers to get down and dirty with the trash!".

Deacon John spins around and knocks Rusty to the ground! He is no longer concerned about witnesses! As he kicks the boy over and over again, the deacon shouts and hisses, "You little candy ass! I've been nothing but kind to you! I pulled you out of the gutter! I gave you a taste of the good life! This is how you repay me? Trying to shame me! Making me out to be some kind of monster!" The big man stops kicking Rusty, backs away and takes a deep breath! Fighting to gain control of the situation, he spits out orders, "Pull yourself together and admit to these boys you are lying!"

I'm speechless! I can't believe what I'm hearing and seeing! It is like watching a scary movie in slow motion! I just want the whole thing to go away and forget it happened!

Rusty is consumed with hatred for his abuser! He feels defiled! He has tried to wash away the awful memories, scrubbing his body so hard it bleeds; washing his clothes in bleach; ironing them at the highest setting! But, nothing works! The stench of Deacon John has permeated his very existence! Nothing makes the pain go away! Nothing blurs the reality of being molested over and over again by the monster that is making a mockery of religion!

Rusty's temper is as explosive as a stick of dynamite! All the anger he has bottled up erupts into a frenzy of emotions! The bruised and beaten boy climbs to his feet, scales a large boulder and lunges at the deacon! Oblivious to the knife in his hand, Deacon John takes a defensive stance! Rusty lands on the blade! The force of his weight propels the deacon backward! He falls to the ground, pinned under the boy! Rusty is motionless!

Claustrophobia overcomes fear! Struggling to breathe, Deacon John pushes the boy aside, rolling his body over and crawling out from under it! He becomes spasmodic and crawls backward on his haunches until his retreat is blocked by a tree! The horrible truth is suddenly exposed! Deacon John's hunting knife is buried in the boy's chest! Dumbfounded, everyone watches in silence as Rusty exhales his final breath!

I can't take my eyes off the body! My heart stops and blood drains from my face! I gasp for air as it starts beating again, pounding in my ears! I look from Jimmy to Steve to Charlie, hoping I've imagine what I've seen! Each face confirms the hard, cold facts! All of us are witness to murder! Steve is the first person to regain his wits. He sprints over to Rusty, kneels down and begins CPR. Although he gets no response, the teenager continues in his efforts. Deacon John pulls him off the lifeless body. He leans down and feels for a pulse. He jerks the knife out of Rusty's body and stands upright. The weapon dangles by his side as the deacon reports, "You're wasting your energy. He's dead."

Dazed and confused, I get up off the ground. Jimmy and Charlie stand up beside me. None of us offer to help him. Instead, we stand paralyzed, looking into the face of a man who has become a very real threat. Deacon John sobs for a few moments. He wipes his eyes with the sleeve of his jacket. He winces and moans, "There's no reason to be afraid of me. Rusty fell on the knife. I didn't stab him on purpose. I didn't mean to kill him."

Steve is aware our survival hangs in the balance. He is frightened but fights his own fear in an effort to protect the rest of the boys. Signaling us with his eyes, Steve agrees with the deranged man. Speaking softly, he says, "We know that. It was a horrible accident."

Deacon John scrutinizes us while he listens to Steve. He sees fear and anger in our eyes. Slowly, it dawns on him that he might have to answer for his crime. He could be ostracized from the church. Worse still, he could actually go to jail. Everything depends on what we say. If our stories differ from his, the deacon will be the one to pay ... not us. As a ploy for sympathy, the wounded man touches his shoulder and shows us the blood on his hand. Getting no reaction, he begins to panic. He protests, "As God is my witness, I would never do the awful things Rusty said. Y'all know he was lying, right?" Looking from one boy to the next, he frets, "Rusty was a sick twisted boy. I should never have pulled him out of the gutter. I should have left him in that cesspool he called home."

The silence is deafening. Determined to win

some sympathy, the deacon declares, "I'm a good man! I'm the victim here ... not Rusty!"

Trying to gain his confidence, Steve lies, "We know that. Don't worry about us."

Glancing at Steve, Deacon John admits, "I had to defend myself." Turning to look at us, he continues, "Y'all saw ..." Without finishing his sentence, he stops talking. He takes a step toward us. We back up. He takes another step forward and we back up again. The deacon realizes he is being duped. He knows his words are falling on deaf ears.

Sensing his anguish and desperation, Steve offers, "Why don't you give me the knife and let me help you?"

Steve's condescending manner is beginning to gall the man. Suspicious of his motives, Deacon John challenges, "Who do you think you are? I'm the adult here ... not you!" Becoming more paranoid, he adds, "Don't treat me like a child or a 'Looney tune.' I'm in control here ... not you!"

****

Battling the thick foliage and rocky terrain, it takes several hours for Deacon John to make it back to the van. Out of breath, he jerks open the door and climbs inside. Covering his face with his hands, the lone man sobs for several minutes. When he quits crying, he wipes his face with the sleeve of his jacket.

Sitting motionless in the truck, Deacon Johns appears to be lost in thought. As the van light shines down on him, he notices the excessive amount of blood on his jacket. He dabs at the stains, gets out of the van and removes his coat. He looks down and focuses on his knife which is secure in its sheath. He pulls it out and stares at the bloody weapon for a few moments.

Deacon John reaches inside the van and turns on the headlights. As he surveys the area. he focuses on a Pine tree directly in front of the vehicle. He walks over to the base of the tree, falls to his knees and thrusts the knife into the earth repeatedly. When the dirt is loose, he uses his hands to scoop it out of the hole. He continues this process until the hole is a sufficient size. He wraps the knife in the jacket and tosses the incriminating evidence into the hole. He uses his hands to scoop the dirt back inside. Then, he stands up and uses his boots to level the ground. After he is satisfied the ground is level, the deacon gathers several piles of leaves and scatters them over the freshly turned earth.

After he surveys the area for a final time. Deacon John returns to the van. He opens the rear door, finds a rag and wipes the mud off his hands. He tosses the rag into the rear compartment, slams the door shut and walks to the driver's side. He climbs inside, retrieves his keys and starts the engine. As he starts to drive away, the deacon realizes his eyeglasses are gone. He searches his pockets before determining they fell off while he was burying his jacket and knife. He considers going back and digging them up but decides to get out of there while the getting is good. He puts the van in gear and drives away.

Chapter 3

Limbo

Deacon John screeches the van to a halt at the entrance of the police station in Boone. He jumps out of the vehicle and runs inside the building. As he enters the lobby, tears flow from his eyes. He sobs, "Help me! Help me! Somebody, please help me!"

Office Matthews is on duty at the Watauga County Sheriff's Office. He rushes to help the distressed stranger and asks, "What in the world happened to you?" Seeing blood, he exclaims, "Oh, my God, you're bleeding! We need to get you to a hospital!"

The stranger waves off his assistance and cries, "You don't get it! It's the boys who need help ... not me!"

Trying desperately to understand the source and assess the situation, Officer Matthews guides the man to a chair and says, "I don't understand! Take a deep breath and calm down! I can't help you or anyone else if I don't have a clue what you're talking about?"

Deacon John plops down in the chair and sobs in his hands. The young officer leaves him sitting alone, goes into a nearby office, picks up the phone and dials. As soon as a voice answers, Deputy Matthews speaks in a low but demanding voice, "You better get over here right now! A man just walked into the building, bleeding and rambling about hurt boys!"

Sheriff James responds, "Take him into my office. Don't let him out of your sight. I'll be there ASAP!"

Straightening his posture, Officer Matthews returns to the lobby. He assumes a professional demeanor and speaks in a firm voice, directing, "Please follow me into the sheriff's office."

Deacon John gets up and walks behind the deputy into the designated area. Sitting down in the nearest chair, he says nothing.

Officer Matthews makes an observation and suggests, "It's a nasty night out there, rain and all. I bet you could use some hot coffee." Without waiting for a response, he walks over to a side table where a pot of coffee sits on a hot plate, He retrieves a cup and fills it with the steamy brew. He carries it across the room and places the cup in the stranger's hand..

Deacon John doesn't look up or comment. He takes a few gulps but makes no attempt to speak or move. Both men remain silent until a man in casual attire bounds into the office. The sheriff looks from the deputy to the large man sitting in the chair. Motioning for his subordinate to remain quiet, Sheriff James stands and observes the mystery man.

Sheriff James is forty-nine years of age. He is a handsome man for his years and possesses a quiet, unassuming manner. Although he projects the image of an uneducated redneck, the sheriff is actually a well-educated, highly competent police official.

In a soothing voice, he says, "I'm Sheriff James. I understand you've been involved in an accident." He pauses before he continues, "You indicated to my deputy that some boys were hurt. Have you calmed down enough to give me some details?"

Deacon John's eyes project a glint of hostility as he announces, "There wasn't any accident! The boys were stabbed to death!" As a look of shock crosses the sheriff's face, the deacon resumes his sad state and adds, "By the grace of God. I barely managed to escape with my life!"

Although he is taken aback by the deacon's revelation, Sheriff James realizes it is imperative to keep the witness calm in order to get answers. He pulls up a chair and sits down across from the deacon. The sheriff grabs an ashtray, removes a pack of cigarettes from his pocket and lights up. In a deliberate effort to form a bond, he offers one to the big man. As the man waves off the gesture, Sheriff James stares at the intruder and urges, "Why don't you start at the beginning?"

Looking down at his hands, the stranger responds, "I'm John Wesley Powers. Everyone calls me, Deacon John.. I teach a Bible Study group for adolescent boys at the First Baptist Church in Asheville. Every year before school starts, I take them on a special outing. This year, we decided to go camping." He pauses for a moment before continuing, "We set up camp in the mountains nearby and had a wonderful afternoon. Four of the boys went fishing while Rusty and I explored the woods."

Sheriff James interrupts, "Why didn't you and Rusty go fishing?

Using his hands to convey his message, the deacon explains, " Rusty was an introvert. He didn't play well with others."

Curious, Sheriff James questions, "If he didn't get along with his peers, why did you bring him?"

Deacon John heaves a long deep sigh and confides, "I felt sorry for him. He kinda reminded me of myself as a child. He was dirt poor. He never knew his dad."

Interrupting his trip down memory lane, Sheriff James directs, "Let's get back on track, shall we?"

Deacon John is silent for a few moments before continuing, "The boys caught some trout. When I gutted one of 'em, I cut my hand. I wrapped it in a handkerchief to keep it from bleeding. We ate our meal A few hours later, we sat by the fire and roasted marshmallows."

Not the least bit interested in petty details, Sheriff James interrupts again by probing, "When did the trouble start?"

Grimacing with pain, the deacon answers, "My hand started bleeding through the bandage. I thought it would be a good idea to go down to the creek and clean it. I was bending over the water when someone pushed me. I fell and hit my head on a rock." He takes a moment to touch the lump on his forehead before continuing, "I must have passed out. A few minutes later, I came to. My head was throbbing. My shoulder was cut and bleeding. I didn't have a clue what happened?"

Deacon John begins to sob. Neither police officer moves or speaks. As soon as he quits crying, the big man offers, "I got up and headed back to camp. When I got there, I saw Steve, Charlie and Rusty lying on the ground, covered in blood. I was so shocked I couldn't move. When I got my wits about me, I checked 'em for a pulse ... all three were dead."

Unable to thoroughly digest the information he is being fed, Sheriff James inquires, "Are you absolutely certain they were dead?"

Looking down at his hands, Deacon John confides, "Yes. I found my father dead in the barn when I was a youngster. I know what death looks like."

Not impressed by his response, Sheriff James argues, "I don't think one encounter with death makes you an expert."

Pleased the sheriff has taken the bait, Deacon John counters, "I agree, but a tour of duty in Vietnam does."

The room is silent for a few moments before the sheriff continues his interrogation, challenging, "I thought there were five boys. What happened to the other two?

Expecting his question, Deacon John recalls, "I looked all over the place but I couldn't find them. I knew I had to get help; so I gave up the search and headed back to my van." He stops talking, lets out a loud cry and gasps, "When I got about halfway down the mountain, I spotted the two of 'em lying at the base of a tree ... they were both dead."

After listening to the deacon's account of the murders, Sheriff James stands up and scrutinizes his superficial wounds. Turning his back to the witness and speaking in a monotone, the sheriff summarizes, "So, let me get your story straight. You and five boys go camping in a remote area of the woods. You cut yourself by accident when you prepare fish for dinner. After dark, you go down to the stream alone to wash your bleeding hand. Someone approaches from behind and pushes you into the creek. You fall into the water, whop your head on a rock and pass out. Your assailant stabs you several times in the back for good measure and leaves you for dead. Then, he scurries back to camp and murders the boys."

Sheriff James turns and glares at the deacon for confirmation. The deacon nods his head. The Sheriff retrieves a cigarette and lights it. Then, he paces the room as he continues with his summary, "When you regain consciousness, you return to camp and find three boys dead, lying in their own blood. You fear for the safety of the other two. You can't find them so you decide to go for help. It is pitch dark and pouring rain. As you backtrack to your car, you find the other two boys dead at the base of a tree."

The sheriff stops pacing and looks intently at the deacon, who is focused on his hands and refuses to meet his gaze. Deacon John validates his conclusions by simply nodding his head. Frustrated by his witness's emotional state, Sheriff James quips, "Feel free to jump in any time and correct me if I'm wrong."

His sarcasm falls on deaf ears. Consequently, the sheriff continues with his summary, " You manage to stagger out of the woods, safe and sound, leaving the bodies of five boys behind." After a moment of silence, the sheriff inquires, "Were you armed?"

Deacon John looks up askance. His response sounds rehearsed as he answers, "I had a hunting knife with me but I lost it."

The sheriff sits down and faces the deacon. He looks directly into the deacon's eyes and asks, "When?"

Meeting his gaze, Deacon John retorts, "If I knew when, I'd know where!" The sheriff arches his brow and frowns. Deacon John appears to think for a moment before adding, "The last time I remember having my knife I was gutting the trout on a big rock. Then, I cut myself. I must've left it there."

Growing suspicious of the deacon, Sheriff James pries, "Are you telling me you went into the woods with five boys armed with one knife?" He gives the deacon a moment to respond before challenging, "Didn't it occur to you a gun might come in handy if you were attacked by wild animals ... or better yet ... a killer on the loose?."

Assuming a pious demeanor, Deacon John reports, "When I got home from Vietnam, I swore I'd never touch a gun again. I put my fate in God's hands."

Overcome with emotion and frustration, Sheriff James pounds his fist on his desk and shouts, "Well, it's a damn shame He wasn't able to protect five innocent children!"

No one moves or speaks for several moments. The silence is deafening. Finally, Sheriff James gets up and stands in front of the deacon, restricting his movements. He peers into his eyes and apologizes,

"Excuse me for my lack of compassion but I'm just a small town cop who isn't in the habit of taking reports of multiple homicides!" He catches his breath before asking, "Do you want to call a lawyer?"

Shocked by his question, Deacon John exclaims, "You're kidding, right?

Looking the deacon directly in the eyes, Sheriff James responds, "I don't joke when murder is on the table."

Insulted by his suspicious mind, Deacon John recoils, "No! I don't want to call a lawyer! I'm a God fearing man! I have nothing to hide!"

Realizing the witness has nothing else to offer, Sheriff James inquires, "Are you ready to take us to the bodies?"

Without needing a moment to consider the option, Deacon John responds, "There is no way I can find the bodies in the dark! And, in case you haven't noticed, I need medical attention!"

Not the least bit surprised by his negative response, Sheriff James concludes, "Since your sense of direction and injuries didn't hinder you from getting out of the woods, I figured they weren't a factor now." Apathetic to the deacon's physical condition, he adds, "My deputy and I will take you to the hospital and have you stitched up." As the men rise to their feet, the sheriff inquires, "Do you have a change of clothes?"

Obviously confused by his question, Deacon John responds, "I might have some clothes in the van. Why?"

The sheriff heaves a long, deep sigh and states, "We'll need your clothes as evidence, including your boots. If you can't find anything to put on, we'll provide something."

Chapter 4

Zack

Standing six-feet-one-inch, Zack poses nude in front of a full-length mirror. He raises his arms and flexes his muscles as he admires his biceps and six-pack. He drops his arms and moves closer to the mirror to focus on his facial features. His thick, ebony hair compliments his long, dark eyelashes and icy blue eyes. His flawlessly fair skin gives prominence to dimples, full lips and perfectly formed teeth. He thinks, *God, I'm a handsome devil.*

As he stands mesmerized by his own reflection, Vicky walks into the bedroom and asks, "Are you enjoying the view?"

Zack smiles into the mirror and answers, "Why shouldn't I? I'm twenty-eight years old, lean, mean and handsome." He pauses before continuing, "Not many men my age have money in the bank, drive a brand-new Porsche, spend their days making love and their nights arresting bad guys."

Vicky straightens the linens and says, "Well, this beautiful twenty-four year old woman, who serves as a punching bag for her husband, needs for you to get dressed and out of here." She sighs and adds, "Seriously, I don't want Jim to catch you naked in our bedroom."

Zack ambles over to the chair and retrieves his briefs and trousers. Moving in slow motion, he steps into his pants and asks, "What would he do if he caught us?"

Vicky stops working and puts her hands on her hips. Frowning, she replies, "After you left, he'd beat the shit out of me!"

Zack raises his brow, stares at Vicky in disbelief and argues, "He wouldn't come after me?"

Vicky shrugs her shoulders as she lights a cigarette. In a trembling voice, she answers, "Jim doesn't fight with men. He prefers the weaker sex."

Vicky scampers around the room putting her personal articles in order. While he buttons his shirt, Zack looks at Vicky and inquires, " Don't you know a woman who cheats on her husband is first cousin to a whore? Maybe, you deserve a good beating."

Vicky is startled and angered by Zack's malicious remark. She stops cleaning the room and stands up straight. In a high-pitched voice, she shrieks, "I knew you were a real son-of-a-bitch pretty boy but I didn't realize you were just another prick!"

Undaunted by her retort, Zack smiles broadly and walks slowly toward the door. In a tiresome voice, he says, "You live and learn, sweetheart. You live and learn."

Zack walks out of the room and closes the door behind him. He hears sobs and the breaking of glass. He gets into his black 1997 Turbo Coupe and starts the engine. He races the motor a few times, presses the clutch, puts the car in gear and merges with traffic. As he drives across town, he thinks about his relationship with Vicky.

Zack met Vicky when he was coming off duty. She was leaving the police station and bumped into him. As he apologized for his clumsiness, her blackened eye and reddish, swollen cheek got his attention. Teary eyed, Vicky nodded and kept on walking. Intrigued by her striking appearance, Zack followed her. As she stepped off the curb, he grabbed her elbow and said, "You look like you could use a cup of coffee and a friend."

Surprised by his forwardness, Vicky stopped in her tracks and stared up at the handsome stranger. Making his move, Zack confided, "I'm Detective Lee. I work in the homicide division but I'm familiar with assault cases. I can offer some good advice if you have time to listen."

Flattered, Vicky blinked her eyes, blushed and replied, "I appreciate all the help I can get. But, I prefer something stronger than coffee."

Pleased with her response, Zack guided the beautiful

woman toward a bar on the next block. After he ordered two Vodka tonics, Vicky shared her private life by saying, "I'm Vicky McGee. My husband's name is Jim. We've been married for two years. At first, our marriage was great. Now, it's a war zone." Zack listened patiently. Vicky went on, "Jin hates his job. He comes home from work looking for an argument. As soon as I open my mouth, he starts slapping me around. Nothing I say makes him happy. Everything I say makes him mad. I'm fed up with trying to appease him."

Curious, Zack asked, "Do you love him? Do you want your marriage to work?"

Vicky answered, "I'm walking that narrow line between love and hate. But, I'd leave him today if I had the money."

Zack asked, "Is that really what you want to do?"

Laughing nervously, Vicky said, "I thought you were a detective ... not a psychologist."

They talked for more than an hour. Vicky went to the police because Jim had hit her one time too many. But, she admitted she didn't have the nerve to press charges. Although he was bored with her sob story, Zack pretended to be interested and concerned about her welfare. When they left the bar, he handed her his card and said, "Call if you need me."

As he strolled toward his car, Zack smiled and thought, God, I'm good! Offer a pretty woman a sympathetic ear and it's only a matter of time before you reap your reward.

As predicted, two days later, Zack received a telephone message from Vicky asking him to come by her house. Zack made a special effort to drop by in the middle of the afternoon.

34

Talking turned to kissing. Kissing led to petting. The result was sexual gratification.

Zack saw Vicky on the sly for a couple of months. When he recognized that loving glint in her eyes, he knew it was time for the relationship to come to an abrupt halt. He had repeated the words many times in the past and his modus operandi never failed. Zack was confident he had accomplished his goal this afternoon by the hurt and anger in Vicky's eyes.

A honking horn and screeching brakes interrupt Zack's daydreaming. He becomes alert and pays attention to his driving. He reaches the police station and maneuvers his sports car into a parking space. Glancing at his watch, he rushes inside the building. Almost immediately, Zack spies Bobby leaning against the wall, waiting for him.

Bobby is Zack's partner, not because he likes him but because Zack is the best detective on the force. He knows he can learn from his cohort; so, he keeps his mouth shut and his eyes and ears open. As they race for the briefing room, Bobby comments, "I'm not going to ask."

Zack winks. The two men sprint down the corridor. When they enter the briefing room, no one looks up and acknowledges their late arrival. Captain Reynolds continues with his instructions to the other officers. After he has informed them of their duties, the captain looks at Zack and Bobby. He inquires, "Have you solved the liquor store shooting?"

Zack answers, "Yep, we'll take the perp into custody later tonight."

Captain Reynolds responds, "Good! I'll expect a full report on my desk by morning." Speaking to the entire group, he orders, "Now get out there and do your jobs."

Captain Reynolds is aware of the differences between Bobby and Zack. Bobby is a good cop. He gets to the station early, stays late, never misses work or comes in with a hangover. His shortcoming is his inability to wade through the evidence and come up with the one clue that will break the case.

Zack is not as straight-laced as Bobby. He drinks too much and has the reputation of being a lady's man. But, he has an uncanny ability to solve crimes. With the nose of a bloodhound, he can find the proverbial *needle in the haystack*. For this reason and this reason alone, the captain gives Zack a longer leash than the other detectives.

The two investigators leave the office and head for their unmarked car. Bobby surrenders to his curiosity and asks, "Okay, who is she?"

Zack laughs and retorts, "You're supposed to be a detective ... detect."

Bobby slams his hand on the steering wheel. Noting his frustration, Zack confides, "Just another horny broad ... the one I talked out of filing assault charges against her husband?"

Bobby arches his brow and recalls, "The good-looking married woman with the black eye?"

Zack shrugs and answers, "Yeah, she needed a shoulder to cry on. Now, she wants a shoulder to lean on." He sighs and continues, "She's good in the sack but I'm a distraction not the cure. So, I broke it off this afternoon."

Frowning, Bobby remarks, "Man, you're the kind of asshole who gives good guys a bad rep!" Glancing at his partner, Bobby warns, "One of these days, you're gonna meet your match and she's gonna break your heart."

Zack flinches as he admits, "My heart was broken before I could walk. There's nothing left to damage."

Zack's tone reveals Bobby has struck a nerve. This is the first time he has ever gotten an emotional reaction from his partner. Although his curiosity is piqued, Bobby changes the subject because his primary concern is for Zack to keep a cool head and watch his back.

The two detectives follow their lead and apprehend their suspect. After filing their report, they call it a night and head out of the building. Making a conscious effort to be congenial, Zack asks, "Do you want to get a drink before heading home?"

Bobby shakes his head and declines, "No thanks, I need to get home to the wife."

Zack gets in his car and heads toward the south side of town. He drives over the Matthews Bridge and exits the freeway. He stops by his habitual late-night bar and has a few glasses of his preferred poison. When the dawn hour approaches, Zack leaves the nightspot and heads home. En route, he listens to the local disc jockey talk about Thanksgiving turkeys.

Zack turns into his driveway and pushes the button to open the double garage door. His two Dobermans race to greet their master. Zack drives into the garage, kills the engine and climbs out of the car. His dogs nuzzle him for attention. He pats Samson and Delilah on their heads and instructs them to follow him into the house.

Zack's home is located on four acres of property heavily grown with giant oak trees draped with Spanish moss. The front lawn is landscaped with a variety of floral bushes accented by large, white rocks. The exterior is composed of brick and stone designed in English Tutor style. French doors and huge windows line the rear portion of the structure. A private dock on the St. John's River secures his speedboat.

An Italian marble floor graces the entrance of the massive two-story home. The main level consists of a living room, dining room, kitchen, den with fireplace, oversized master bedroom and two bathrooms. The upper level contains four bedrooms and two baths. The furnishings are tastefully displayed having been selected under the artistic guise of a pricey interior decorator.

After devouring a TV dinner, feeding and watering the dogs, Zack walks into the den and plops down in his leather chair. He turns on the television, hits the mute button and watches the sports channel. Zack notices the button flashing on the telephone recorder and presses it.

Talking into the recording device, a female voice says, "This is Aunt Ruth. I want to remind you we'll be having Thanksgiving dinner at precisely four o'clock. Please come! We've missed you. Bye, Zack darling."

Zack leans back in the recliner and closes his eyes. Ruth's message sends his mind reeling backward in time.

Zack's first image is Jack. Born in Charlotte, North Carolina on October 4, 1970, Zack came first and Jack was born five minutes later. Their parent, Eleanor and Eric Lee, were overjoyed with the arrival of their identical twins.

Eric was a corporate executive for an international banking firm. Eleanor was a socialite mom. Being the product of a wealthy family, she considered social functions an integral part of her life. Seen at all the right places at the appropriate times, Eleanor hired a live-in nanny to care for her young sons.

After the birth of her boys, Eleanor suffered from postpartum depression. She started her days with a Bloody Mary and ended them with Scotch on the Rocks. No one appeared to notice her alcoholism or dared mention it. Because of her drunken tantrums, the nannies came and went as often as her shopping sprees.

Zack and Jack were inseparable. Verbal communication wasn't necessary. Each one knew instinctively what the other wanted. Sadly, the special love they shared ended abruptly when tragedy tore them apart.

On July 18, 1974, the twin boys were playing outside near the pool area. The nanny was chatting on the telephone in broken English. Eleanor lay in a drunken stupor inside the house. Somehow, Jack managed to squeeze through the gate opening, which restricted the swimming pool. Zack tried to follow but was too large to squirm inside. In a matter of minutes, he watched his brother tumble and fall into the pool!

Zack ran to the nanny for help! She shooed him away! He scurried into the house to arouse his mother! She couldn't or wouldn't open her eyes! He ran back outside, looked through the wood slates and couldn't see his brother! He sat down and screamed until his voice went hoarse! At last, the nanny came over to comfort him! Through his sobs, Zack was able to communicate to his caretaker that Jack had fallen into the water!

The nanny panicked and bolted through the gate! The domestic screamed in horror when she saw Jack's body at the bottom of the pool! Unable to swim, she ran into the house to fetch his mother! In seconds, both women raced past Zack! Eleanor dove into the pool and pulled Jack up from the deep end!

While Eleanor gave Jack mouth-to-mouth resuscitation, the nanny called 9-1-1. Paramedics arrived and attempted to resuscitate the young boy. When they carried his small limp body away on the stretcher wearing an oxygen mask, Zack knew instinctively his brother was dead.

Eleanor faulted the nanny. The nanny pointed her finger at Eleanor. Eric blamed himself for being away from home. Zack held each and every one of them accountable.

The nanny was fired on the spot. Ruth, Eleanor's sister, was notified of the tragedy and flew in from Florida. During her extended stay, she attended to the family's needs. After a reasonable time of grieving, Ruth returned home and Eric resumed his work habits. Feeling abandoned and guilty, Eleanor plummeted into the depths of despair, numbing her pain with pills and alcohol.

One night when Eric was away on a business trip, Eleanor tiptoed into Zack's bedroom and showered her son with hugs and kisses. She sat in the chair, rocking and watching him sleep. The hour grew late. Eleanor got up, went into her bedroom and shot herself in the heart with her pearl handled revolver.

After his wife's death, Eric became obsessed with Zack. He limited his traveling but still made occasional business trips. On September 12, 1976, Eric departed for London to offset an impending financial disaster. Two hours after departure, his corporate jet exploded over the Atlantic Ocean.

Ruth was notified for a second time. She caught the first plane to Charlotte to take custody of Zack. She accepted his guardianship with a loving and positive spirit. Unbeknownst to her nephew, Ruth deposited his inheritance into an account bearing his name.

Ruth's character was of a different nature entirely from her sister. Married to a state senator, she attended the necessary political functions but had no weakness for alcohol. Nevertheless, *her physical features bore a striking resemblance to Eleanor. This had a traumatic impact on little Zack. Still blaming his mother for Jack's death, Zack transferred his anger and bitterness to Ruth. He never allowed himself to feel any sentimental attachment for her. Moreover, he kept his emotions in check at school and refused to make friends.*

When he was a sophomore in high school, an insightful coach managed to channel his anger into athletic aggression. Zack became captain of the football team. He was popular with the teenage students despite his obnoxious and hateful disposition. The boys respected his sportsmanship. The girls gravitated toward his good looks.

During his senior year, Zack was attracted to the head cheerleader. Sandy was a beautiful young girl with a sparkling, vivacious personality. She fell hopelessly in love with him. After months of kissing and petting, she lost her virginity to her handsome boyfriend. Sandy wanted to marry Zack and be the mother of his children. He had different plans. Zack wanted to go to college and become an FBI agent.

Two weeks before graduation, Sandy told Zack she was pregnant. He was shocked and denied responsibility. Making it crystal clear he wasn't going to be burdened by a wife and child, Zack suggested her best choice of action was an abortion. Sandy was devastated. She cried and begged Zack to reconsider. Her tears were ignored. Her pleas fell on deaf ears. The embittered teenager told her to deal with the matter herself and not bother him with the details. Shortly after graduation, Sandy left Jacksonville and moved to southern Florida. She mailed Zack a letter informing him of her whereabouts. He tossed the envelope in the trash.

Zack went on to Florida State. After a couple of years of college life, he returned home and got a job with the local police department. In an amazingly short period of time, he was promoted to detective. Having recently applied for a position with the State Bureau of Investigation, his ultimate dream is finally beginning to materialize. He is anxiously waiting to hear back from the agency.

Samson licks his master's hand and interrupts his reverie. The dogs need to go outside. Zack gets up and lets them out through the French doors. He follows them down to the river and watches his faithful companions frolic in the grass. Zack considers his pets the perfect choice. Samson is all bark and no bite. Delilah acts humble but won't hesitate to attack. Neither dog requires pampering and both are content to sleep on the floor beside his bed. Zack calls his animals back into the house. Without bothering to undress, he walks into the bedroom, turns off the lights and falls on the bed. As he drifts off to sleep, he thinks, *God, I hate the Holidays.*

Chapter 5

Missing

Zack calls Aunt Ruth early the next morning and declines her invitation to Thanksgiving dinner. He uses the excuse he has to work over the holidays due to shortage of personnel. His aunt isn't surprised. She has heard the same excuse for the past three years. She wishes her nephew a happy holiday. He echoes her kind words of affection.

The Friday after Thanksgiving at approximately eight o'clock pm, the dispatcher breaks the silence in the police vehicle. A woman's voice says, "Head over to Orange Park Mall, pronto. The child of a prominent family has been reported missing. Captain Reynolds wants you two to take the report."

Bobby picks up the mike and responds, "Ten four. We're on our way."

Zack turns on the siren, floors the gas pedal and races to the shopping center. When the two plain-clothes detectives reach the mall entrance, a uniformed officer directs them to the office. As soon as they walk through the door, an overwrought woman accosts them.

The hysterical woman appears to be about thirty-two years of age. She stands five feet five inches and is slender in build. She has dark hair and brown eyes. Although her features are rather plain, it is apparent she is a socialite by the design of her clothes. Having no sense of diplomacy, the high society female demands attention rather than asking for it.

The protagonist confronts Zack and screams, "You find my daughter right now! She was by my side one moment and gone the next! I demand you close this mall and find her!"

Bobby attempts to calm her fears. In a soothing voice, he says, "I'm Detective Johnson. This is my partner, Detective Lee. I realize you are extremely upset; but screaming and yelling won't help us find your little girl."

Zack crosses his arms over his chest and faces the hostile witness. He takes a deep breath and explains, "We're all on the same team here. We need for you to calm down and cooperate. Take a deep breath and tell us everything we need to know to find your little girl."

The frantic woman collapses into a nearby chair. Between words, she gasps, "I'm Mimi Von Haven. I brought my daughter to the mall. I selected a Christmas gift and paid the clerk. When I turned around to take her hand, she was gone."

Zack asks, "Do you have a picture? Can you describe her clothing?"

Mimi begins searching in her purse and frets, "I think I have a picture in my wallet." As she continues to dig for her billfold, she recalls, "Let me think ... she was wearing a green jacket, red sweater with embroidered flowers, blue jeans and tennis shoes. Yes, that's what she had on ... and red socks."

With shaky hands, Mimi retrieves a photograph of her daughter and hands it to Zack. As he takes the picture, Zack notes two of the woman's freshly manicured, red fingernails are broken. He looks at the photo, hands it to a uniformed officer and instructs, "Make copies of this. Distribute them throughout the mall. Have officers show this picture to as many shoppers and clerks as possible."

Zack turns his attention back to Mimi. He meets her gaze and studies her expression. He recognizes the look of fear but he also perceives a glint of guilt. Zack backs away and scrutinizes the woman's appearance. He notices dirty smudges on her hemline and several runs in her hose. The fact that her shoes are pristine and out of sync with the rest of her apparel strikes him as odd. Looking up and focusing on Mimi's eyes, Zack suggests, "I'm sure your little girl is just lost. There is no reason to be overly concerned at this point in time. We'll find her ..."

Glaring at Zack, Mimi jumps out of her chair and

screams, "My little girl has a name! It's Mitzi! It is easy for you to be calm! Your daughter isn't missing!"

Zack backs away. Distracting the extremely agitated woman, Bobby gently touches her arm and inquires, "Have you advised your husband of Mitzi's disappearance?"

Mimi starts hyperventilating. Gasping for air she cries, "My God, I didn't even think to call Richard!" She turns, looks frantically at the mall manager and pleads, "Would you call him? I'm too upset."

Before he has a chance to respond, Mimi scribbles the phone number down on a pad, lying on the desk. The unidentified employee waits patiently for her to finish writing. He picks up the slip of paper and walks into his office. He is seen dialing the phone through the glass partition.

Bobby proceeds to get pertinent details concerning her lifestyle. Afterwards, he turns to a uniformed officer and orders, "Get a list of Mrs. Von Haven's family, friends and possible enemies." Then, he turns back to Mimi and states, "Mrs. Von Haven, Detective Lee and I will be leading the investigation. We need to leave now and join the search."

Dazed and confused, Mimi focuses on Zack and asks, "What am I supposed to do? Should I wait here or go home?"

Straightening his posture, Zack responds, "You should stay here for at least another hour. If Mitzi hasn't been found in that length of time, an officer will escort you home." He pauses, takes a breath and adds, "If we haven't located her by eleven, Detective Johnson and I will come by your home and report our findings."

Mimi stands silent as Zack and Bobby leave the room. As soon as they are alone, Bobby asks, "What do you think?"

Zack shrugs his shoulders and answers, "I don't think Mrs. Von Haven is being totally honest."

Bobby is exacerbated by Zack's negative response. He exclaims, "What did she say or do to make you question her honesty? My God! Her daughter is missing! She is desperate to find her! Do you hate women so much you think all of them are liars? Did it even cross your mind she might be telling the truth?"

Angry, Zack gets red-faced. Taking a defensive stance, he retaliates, "No, I don't think all women are liars. But, a helluva lot of 'em twist the truth to suit their purpose."

The two detectives walk in silence toward the exit. Zack spots a plain-clothes detective, stops him and barks, "Put officers at every entrance and interrogate anybody who enters or leaves the mall. Talk to as many shoppers as possible. See if anyone noticed the little girl." He takes a breath and continues, "Find the clerk who sold Mrs. Von Haven her purchase. Confirm whether or not she saw the child."

When they get to their car, Zack picks up the mike and calls dispatch. He instructs, "Get me the home address of Richard Von Haven."

Starting the engine, Zack waits for a response. The dispatcher voice comes back on the speaker with the information. Zack advises, "Ten four. We're en route to that location."

Bobby questions, "You told Mrs. Von Haven we'd be there at eleven?"

Smiling maliciously, Zack replies, "I lied. I want to talk to the babysitter before she does."

Zack pulls their unmarked car into the driveway of a massive white stucco house of Spanish design. The two detectives walk up to the front entrance and ring the bell. They wait in silence until the babysitter opens the door.

As the caretaker blocks the entrance, Zack and Bobby show their badges. Zack begins, "I'm sorry to bother you, ma'am, but Mrs. Von Haven has experienced a slight problem at the mall. Nothing of great concern but we'd like to ask you a few questions."

The babysitter looks worried but not alarmed. She leads the two men into the living room and invites them to take a seat. Before she can speak, Zack states, "Mrs. Von Haven lost Mitzi at the mall. She called the police and officers are presently assisting her in finding the child." As the babysitter catches her breath, Zack inquires, "May I ask your name and position?"

The babysitter is in her mid fifties. She is matronly in appearance. Leaning forward in her seat, she answers, "I'm Claire Winters. I keep the children when Mrs. Von Haven is away from home."

Zack quizzes, "How many children do the Von Havens have?"

Mrs. Winters reports, "Two. Mitzi and the baby, Ricky."

Bobby interrupts and inquires, "Where is Ricky now?"

Mrs. Winters looks puzzled but answers, "He is upstairs in his crib sleeping." Getting concerned, she asks, "I thought you knew this already? Why so many questions?

Zack leans forward and pats Mrs. Winters on the hand in a reassuring manner. He answers, "We knew about Mitzi, but we weren't informed about the baby." After a moment of silence, he inquires, "Why are you sitting for the Von Havens tonight?

Mrs. Winters is quick to respond, "The housekeeper stays until six. I come when she leaves but today was a little different."

Trying to conceal his heightened interest, Bobby shifts his weight and pries, "How so?"

Noting his change in demeanor, Mrs. Winters enunciates her words and answers, "Mrs. Von Haven called me at three. She said the maid had to leave early and she needed me desperately. She begged me to come over right away." She stops talking, takes a deep breath and continues, "I told her I'd get there as soon as possible. Then, I hung up the phone."

Zack looks at his watch to put emphasis on the time factor. He asks, "What time did you get here?"

The babysitter looks at her watch to compare time. Wanting to emphasize her answer is an estimate, she replies, "I got here about four-thirty or thereabouts. I'm not certain as to the exact time."

Bobby asks, "What happened when you got here?"

Mrs. Winters sighs and responds, "Mrs. Von Haven had calmed down considerably. She told me Ricky was asleep. Then, she informed me she and Mitzi were going to the mall. She left right away."

Zack moves closer to the babysitter, looks into her eyes and prods, "What do you mean she left? I thought Mitzi was with her?"

The babysitter becomes thoughtful. She stares into space for a few moments before answering the question. In a hollow voice, Mrs. Winters reports, "Oh, she was."

Zack has a puzzled look on his face. He holds eye contact with the witness and prompts, "You saw them leave together?"

The babysitter looks stumped. She rests her chin

on her hands and puts her index fingers over her mouth. Then, she declares, "I didn't actually see them leave together if that's what you're asking. Mitzi was in the car."

Bobby presses, "Did you see Mitzi in the car?"

Getting a little confused, Mrs. Winters responds, No, I didn't see her. The car was in the garage. Mrs. Von Haven told me Mitzi was waiting in the car. I assumed that was why she was in such a rush."

The two detectives get up and walk toward the door. Mrs. Winters follows closely on their heels. Acting as though he has an afterthought, Zack turns to look at the babysitter and adds, "Please don't mention to the Von Havens we were here asking questions. They're upset enough. We don't want to cause them any unnecessary worry, do we?"

Mrs. Winters nods her head in agreement. Zack and Bobby leave the house. As they drive away, Bobby confides, "I'm getting a little suspicious myself. It really bothered me when Mrs. Von Haven used the past tense to describe Mitzi's clothes." He sighs and adds, "I hope we're just a couple of paranoid cops."

Zack glances over at Bobby and responds, "Me too."

Zack and Bobby head to the police station. Captain Reynolds listens to their report and surmises. "No one gave an eye witness account of seeing the child. The sales clerk didn't notice her but felt it was due to the swarm of customers looking for holiday sales. Mitzi is still missing and the mall is empty." He stops talking, focuses on Zack and asks, "What's your gut feeling?"

Zack leans on the back of a chair and flexes his hands. He inhales deeply and responds, "Something's not right. I can feel it. When we got to the mall office, Mrs. Von Haven was hostile one minute and cooperative the next. Her pupils were dilated, her hands shook and I caught a whiff of Vodka on her breath." He pauses before going on, "She was mad as Hell but I'm not sure if she was mad at the child, herself or us? There was a look in her eyes that chilled me to the bone. I can't explain it."

Captain Reynolds raises his eyebrow and confides, "I'm listening."

Zack walks around the chair and sits down. He appears to be talking as much to himself as the captain. He deduces, "Mrs. Von Haven claims she spent the morning at the beauty shop. If that's the truth, she should go back and demand a refund because her hair looked like shit. Two of her freshly manicured nails were broken and jagged at the tips. The lower portion of her skirt was spattered with mud. Thorns were caught in her hemline. Her stockings were run but her shoes looked pristine.?" He catches his breath and continues, "The babysitter said Mrs. Von Haven took the child to the mall but she didn't see the child before they left."

Bobby has a knee-jerk reaction to Zack's power of observation and questions, "How did you notice all those details? I didn't see anything but a panic-stricken mother." Noting the captain's look of disapproval, he rebounds, "But, the fact she spoke of her daughter in the past tense bothered me."

Captain Reynolds sits down at his desk. After taking a few moments to digest the input, he admits, "I hope your suspicious mind is playing tricks on you. But, I don't understand why no one noticed the little girl? You would think at least one person saw her?"

The small office is quiet for a few minutes. Everyone focuses on his own thoughts. Breaking the silence, Captain Reynolds warns, "Tread carefully. Follow all the legal procedures to the letter. Get back to work and solve this case."

Around eleven, Zack and Bobby return to the Von Haven residence. They are greeted by a police officer standing guard at the door. After flashing their badges, the two detectives enter the house. They find Mimi and Richard Von Haven sitting on the couch in the living room. Dabbing her tears, Mimi nods. Richard stands up and extends his hand.

Richard appears to be in his early forties. He is six feet three inches and his weight is proportionate to his height. His hair is brown and graying at the temples. His eyes are emerald green and bloodshot. He possesses the demeanor of a corporate executive. Although he moves and speaks like a diplomat, the wrinkles on his brow indicate he takes life very seriously. The worried father looks at the two detectives and asks, "Did you find Mitzi?"

Shaking hands, Zack answers, "No sir, but the entire police force is searching for her."

Richard pats Mimi on the shoulder. Then, he motions for the two detectives to follow him. When they are alone, Richard whispers, "My wife is in a very fragile mental state. She has been suffering from postpartum depression. In fact, she's under the care of a physician. Tonight, we were going to a party at ..."

Suddenly, Richard realizes he is rattling on about trivial matters. He stops talking and looks intently from Zack to Bobby. In a trembling voice, he asks, "Do you have any idea where my daughter is?"

Bobby straightens his posture. He looks directly into Richard's eyes and explains, "We're working on the theory she is lost. Somebody might have taken her home, hoping to locate her parents. Or, she could be wandering around the mall area." He takes a breath and continues. "On a positive note, it's not a rough neighborhood and most of the shoppers live close by."

Fighting to control his fear, Richard listens to Bobby. Speaking in a hushed tone, he admits, "I don't think Mimi could handle the loss of Mitzi. I'm afraid it would kill her or drive her over the edge. Quite frankly, I don't know how I'd handle it myself."

Zack shifts his weight to get Richard's attention. Speaking with deliberate control, he says, "I don't mean to offend you but I'm forced by my position as an officer of the law to ask you a few questions which have to be answered." He stares at Richard and continues, "Has your wife ever caused injury to herself or your children?"

Richard steps backward as though the words are a physical blow. As his eyes blaze with anger, he gasps, "If you're suggesting Mimi ever attempted suicide, the answer is NO! More to the point, Mimi has never so much as raised a hand against me or our children!" He stops talking, takes a gulp of air and finishes, "Does that answer your question, detective?"

Bobby steps forward to defend his partner's position. He counters, "You just said your wife lapsed into a deep depression after the birth of your son. So deep, in fact, she is under a doctor's care." As the muscles in Richard's face twitch, Bobby continues, "I'm sorry sir; but at the present time, we're more concerned with your daughter's whereabouts than your wife's mental state."

Listening to Bobby's logic, Richard's rage dissipates. He takes a deep breath and admits, "You're right, Detective. Mitzi is the most important person in the world at this critical time." He turns to face Zack and apologizes, "I'm sorry for my outburst. Please find my daughter and bring her home."

Zack nods as he replies, "We'll do our best. We are already searching the area surrounding the mall.

And, with your permission, we need to install a tap on your phone in the event Mitzi has been kidnapped."

Richard's mouth falls open. He gasps for air and leans against the wall for support. Struggling to speak, he whispers, "Do you think she's been kidnapped?"

Zack offers his arm for support. Talking in a soothing voice, he answers, "No sir. Mitzi was in her mother's custody when she went missing. She is big enough to have screamed and resisted if a stranger grabbed her. Even if someone overpowered her, there were too many customers around for such a scene to have gone unnoticed."

Bobby interrupts, "Sir, we need to join the search team. We'll advise you as soon as we have any leads."

Zack and Bobby leave the residence and join the search. They look all night and into the morning. Everyone calls Mitzi's name. They knock on doors, interview people on the street and canvas the nearby woods. There is no sign of the little girl.

Chapter 6

Murder

Shortly before noon on Saturday, Zack and Bobby sit in their car, studying a city map. The dispatcher comes on the radio and reports, "A child's body has been spotted behind a vacant house in Riverside Heights. The address is One thirteen River Road. Proceed there immediately."

Bobby frowns at Zack and picks up the mike. He responds, "Ten Four. We're on our way."

Zack and Bobby arrive at the scene and see officers roping off the area. They get out of their car and head toward the back of the house. A uniformed officer joins them, refers to his notes and reports, "A fisherman spotted an unusual object near the shoreline. He drove his motorboat close enough to determine it was a body. He sped away to the closest dock and called the police. When we arrived at his location, he led us here. He is being questioned by another officer as we speak."

Lying partially submerged and face down in the shallow water, Zack and Bobby spot the little girl's body. Mitzi is wearing the clothes her mother described. Both men watch in silence as the medical examiner approaches carrying his black satchel. When the forensic expert begins to examine the small, lifeless form, Zack instructs, "Run the test to see if the child has been sexually assaulted."

The medical examiner conducts his preliminary examination. Immediately afterward, he signals the waiting attendants to remove the body. Mitzi is placed on a stretcher, put in the ambulance and transported to the city morgue.

Zack watches the emergency vehicle disappear before going into action. In a husky voice, he orders, "Bobby, concentrate your search here. I'm going to scope out the area near the driveway."

Bobby nods his head and uses the location of Mitzi's body as his pivot point. Zack walks back to the driveway. Both investigators bend up and down, sift sand through their fingers and move slowly toward each other. Bobby finds a small shrub bearing thorns. He breaks off a sample and deposits it in a plastic bag. He swoops up some mud and pours it into another plastic container.

Zack inches around the edge of the driveway. He uses his shoes to scatter the surface dirt. For nearly an hour, he stoops over and surveys the ground, zigzagging back and forth as he moves toward Bobby's location. A glare catches his eye. He kneels and finds the source. He reaches into his pocket, gets a plastic bag, retrieves the evidence and drops it inside. Then, he rises to his feet and hollers, "We've got what we came for! Let's go!"

Bobby gets off his knees, stands up and looks at Zack. Jogging over to his partner, he asks, "Why do you look like the cat that swallowed the Canary?"

Zack holds up his bag, shows Bobby its contents and says, "It gives me some degree of satisfaction to know the murderer isn't going to get away with her crime."

Bobby examines the evidence, frowns and asks, "How are we going to approach the Von Havens?"

Zack kicks the sand with his shoe, glances at Bobby and answers, "We're going to take Mr. Von Haven to the morgue and ask him to identify the body. Then, we'll send him home. As soon as we get the lab results, you and me are going to the arrest his wife."

******

It is Monday, December 1, late in the afternoon. Mimi has been arrested, booked and fingerprinted. She is escorted into the interrogation room where her attorney sits waiting. He rises and helps his client to a chair. The uniformed officer leaves the room when Zack and Bobby enter. The attorney whispers to Mimi and pats her hand.

Mimi's attorney, fifty-three years of age, is the

epitome of distinction. Piercing green eyes, gray hair and a professionally trimmed moustache flatter his tall, lean frame. He wears an expensive suit, custom designed to accentuate his flair for courtroom dramatics. In a firm voice, he instructs, "Mimi, I suggest you sit quietly while these detectives tell us why you are being charged?"

Considering him transparent in design and purpose, Zack ignores the lawyer. He stands, focuses on Mimi and asks, "Mrs. Von Haven, would you care to make a statement concerning the death of your daughter?"

Mimi looks at her lawyer and is prompted to remain silent. She shakes her head, no. Bobby takes a seat at the table, across from Mimi and her attorney. Zack continues to stand as he comments, "These past few days have been extremely difficult. We can drag this morbid case out or wrap it up with the least amount of pain." He pauses and focuses on Mimi before asking, "What are your thoughts?"

Mimi doesn't move or speak. Her attorney looks from Zack to Bobby and appears totally confused. He replies, "I have no idea what you're talking about? Please state your case."

Zack pulls out a small pad and refers to his notes. He reads, "Mrs. Von Haven called the police on Friday evening, November 28, 1997, around seven-thirty pm to report her daughter missing …"

After recounting the facts, Zack removes three plastic bags from a cardboard box marked Von Haven file. He holds up the appropriate bag as he speaks, "This is a mud sample found near Mitzi's body. These are thorns found growing in the same location. These are two broken, red nail tips found near the driveway."

Mimi looks down at her hands, sees her broken nails and gasps! She catches her breath and cries, "I didn't even notice my nails were chipped! I've been so upset about Mitzi I haven't looked at my hands." She stops and inhales deeply. In a trembling voice, she whispers, "I must've broken them when I went to the mall."

Mimi's attorney is surprised by her reaction. Trying to conceal his concern, he pats her hand and instructs, "Mrs. Von Haven, I advise you to remain silent."

Zack retrieves a large brown bag out of the box. He places the bag on the table, opens it and pulls out a red skirt. He points to the mud spots and thorns, attached to the hemline. He tosses the skirt aside and withdraws a pair of muddy tennis shoes. He watches Mimi's reaction. After focusing on his suspect for a few moments, he announces, "My detectives found these items at your house earlier today. The skirt was in the dirty clothes hamper. The shoes were in the trunk of your car." He pauses for a moment before adding, "Mrs. Von Haven, Detective Johnson and I are going to give you a few minutes alone to confer with your lawyer."

Zack gestures for Bobby to join him. He opens the door and follows Bobby out. They walk directly into the adjoining room and peer through the one-way glass partition. Mimi and her lawyer huddle together. His body language indicates he disagrees with his client. Zack and Bobby watch and wait for ten minutes before returning.

As soon as they enter the room, Mimi's attorney looks up and acknowledges them. He frowns and announces, "Mrs. Von Haven wants to make a statement. I have advised her against it but she insists."

Zack and Bobby take seats at the table across from Mimi and her attorney. Mimi dabs at her tears, gulps in air and gasps, "I went to the beauty shop early Friday morning. I had my hair and nails done. Afterwards, I ran some errands and lost track of time. I got home about three." Mimi pauses for a moment before continuing, "The maid was scheduled to leave at two. She was waiting at the door mad as Hell! She went out faster than I came in!"

Mimi stops talking and appears dismayed at having to repeat the bothersome details. Finally, she goes on, "I was so upset. I needed help getting ready for our party and she just left me in the lurch. I called the babysitter and asked her to come over immediately. She promised to come as soon as possible."

Mimi takes a deep breath and seems to be calming down. Then, she starts reliving the experience, mentally and verbally. She begins, "I was standing in my closet taking party dresses off the rack. The baby started crying. I went into the nursery and tried to hush him. Suddenly, I realized Mitzi was nowhere in sight. I called her name but apparently she didn't hear me. I laid the baby down in his crib and went looking for her."

Mimi stops talking. Tears well in her eyes and she starts crying. In a sobbing voice, she confesses, "I found Mitzi in the bathroom sitting in a tubful of water. I got angry and ordered her out of the tub. She started laughing as she splashed water all over the floor. I grabbed a towel, got on my knees and started wiping it up. When I began fussing at her, Mitzi threw water on me, soaking my face and hair."

Mimi's voice chokes. Tears roll down her cheeks. She reaches for the box of Kleenex sitting on a corner of the table. She begins wiping away her tears as she goes on, "I just lost it! I screamed at the top of my lungs! I jumped up, grabbed Mitzi by the arms and started shaking her! The shaking turned to slapping!" She gurgles and catches her breath. Words tumble out of her mouth, "Mitzi got frightened! She started fighting back, screaming and flailing her arms and legs! She even tried to bite me! Everything went black!"

Mimi sits upright in her chair. Tears stream down her cheeks. Patting her hand, the lawyer tries to comfort her. Bobby looks sympathetic. Zack shows no sign of emotion. Mimi gasps, "It was dreamlike. One moment, I was engulfed in darkness. The next second, I was in the light. When my eyes focused, I saw Mitzi in the tub. Her body was perfectly still. Her head was under water. Her eyes were blank."

No one talks for several minutes as the three men envision the horror Mitzi must have experienced in the final moments of her life. When the stupor passes, Zack nudges Bobby with his foot. Bobby moves forward in his seat and prods, "What did you do then?"

Mimi shoves her lawyer's hand off her arm and shrugs. She straightens her posture and answers, "I picked up the towel and got Mitzi out of the tub. I carried her into her bedroom, laid her on the bed and dressed her in her favorite outfit." She swallows and admits, "I carried her downstairs and out into the garage. I put her in the backseat of my car. Then, I went back inside and cleaned up the bathroom."

Mimi heaves a sigh of relief and looks around the room for signs of sympathy. As the men sit spellbound, she continues, "I heard Ricky stirring in his crib. I went into the nursery to check on him. He was fast asleep. I stood there for a few minutes and watched him. Then, I went into my dressing room and fixed my hair and makeup." She catches her breath before finishing, "I changed clothes and went downstairs. Then, I fixed myself a drink and waited for Mrs. Winters."

Zack gets up from his chair and looks down at Mimi waiting for her to continue. She remains mute. He breaks the silence by asking, "What did you do when she arrived?"

Without batting an eyelid, Mimi stares into space and responds, "I knew I had to have an excuse for leaving the house in such a hurry. So, I told her Mitzi and I were going to the mall to buy a present. Then, I rushed out of the house before she had a chance to ask me any questions."

Zack is getting angrier by the second. He scowls as he probes, "And?"

Mimi looks at Zack as though she is looking at him for the first time. She studies his features and replies, "I rode around for a little while, thinking about what I'd done. I got frightened. I didn't want to get caught with my daughter's dead body in the car." She starts to get up from her chair but her attorney puts his hand on her shoulder to hold her in place. She pushes his hand away and recalls, "I remembered seeing a house for sale on the river. I knew it was empty. I drove over there and pulled in the driveway. I didn't see anybody so I parked behind the house. I got Mitzi out of the backseat, carried her to the riverbank and laid her face down in the water."

Bobby interrupts by asking, "How did you happen to have a change of shoes in the car?"

Mimi glances at him as she responds, "I always keep a change of shoes in the car." Bobby looks puzzled. Mimi explains, "My high heels sometimes hurt my feet; so I keep a pair of tennis shoes in the car."

Bobby stares at the woman with a blank expression on his face. His lack of sympathy annoys her and she recoils, " It's not like I planned it, hiding Mitzi's body and all! I couldn't carry her in the sand wearing high heels. The tennis shoes were already in the car."

Zack stares at Mimi in disbelief. He gives her a few moments to show remorse. As she sits like a child in trouble waiting to be punished, Zack inquires, "Is that all? Is there anything else you would like to add?"

Mimi looks up at Zack as though he hurt her feelings. She is totally oblivious to the fact she is the culprit. Insulted by his lack of compassion, Mimi tries to put him on a guilt trip by whimpering, "You're looking at me as though I'm some kind of monster! I didn't mean to kill my little girl! It was an accident!"

Zack takes a step backward. Then, he lunges forward and grabs onto the table so tightly his knuckles turn white. He leans close to Mimi and hisses, "Don't look to me for absolution! If I had my way, I'd strap you in the electric chair and cackle when I pulled the switch!"

Bobby and Mimi's lawyer are mortified by Zack's malice and threatening stance. Bobby jumps up and moves close to his partner as the lawyer shields Mimi with his arm. Mimi pulls away from him, jumps up and confronts Zack.

In a gut wrenching voice, she sobs, "Why do you hate me so much? It wasn't my fault I couldn't control my temper! My doctor keeps me so doped on tranquilizers, half the time I don't know if I'm coming or going!"

Zack retaliates with a vengeance! He comes so close to Mimi their noses almost touch. His words reverberate in the small room as he shouts, "All you rich bitches are the same! You demand everything and give nothing in return! Men have to keep you on a pedestal or there is Hell to pay!" He catches his breath and snarls, "You have to be the center of attention! You have babies and expect the hired help to raise them! And, when something goes terribly wrong, someone else has to take the blame ... the booze, the pills, the help, whatever is handy!"

Everyone is dumfounded. Zack glances at Bobby and the attorney searching for some hint of support. Then the absence of reason ignites again! Zack picks up the nearest chair and hurls it against the wall! He heads for the door, stops and turns to face his nemesis one more time. He points his finger at Mimi and hisses, "DAMN YOU TO HELL!"

Zack storms out of the room! He passes Captain Reynolds in the hall and ignores him. He exits the building, gets in his car, revs the engine and burns rubber as he speeds out of the parking lot!

Chapter 7

Walking In

Zack grabs a bottle of Jack Daniels out of his glove box. He takes a swig and merges with traffic. Tears well in his eyes and cloud his vision. He doesn't see the red light or the car in the intersection. He is oblivious to brakes screeching, metal crushing and glass shattering.

Unaware of the swarm of witnesses rushing to his aid, Zack drifts in and out of consciousness. The 'jaws of life' pry him out of his totaled Porsche. Paramedics strap him to a gurney. The emergency attendants lift his body into the back of an ambulance and speed to the hospital. Trying desperately to revive his patient, the young medic talks nonstop and keeps the driver posted on Zack's condition. Alarmed, he reports, "I'm not getting a pulse or heartbeat!"

Zack finds himself floating above the ambulance, looking down at his own body. He watches as the color drain from his face; lips turn blue. He hears the emergency attendant's voice as he struggles to revive his patient. All the while, Zack has no sense of pain or remorse. Abruptly, he is sucked into a tunnel. As he flails his arms, he senses a void and surrenders to the experience. The spiritual vacuum carries him in an upward spiral until the current stops. Instantly, Zack is spit out of the vortex. He lands on his feet and is blinded by light.

Undulating, translucent hues of white and gold fill the space. A celestial being appears and takes his hand. As she communicates telepathically, the Angel guides Zack toward a pulsating sphere of energy. Zack hears her words in his head, instructing, *Focus your eyes and see what appears before you.* Peering into the circle of life, Zack views his past:

Jack and Zack are toddler, playing and laughing. He spots his mother and father standing aside, smiling at their mischief. A gray cloud casts an ominous shadow on the viewing. With tears in his eyes, Zack witnesses the death of his brother, the suicide of his mother and the accident that robs his father of life. He sees Aunt Ruth cry as he bullies the children at school, walks away from his responsibility to Sandy and drops out of college. He sees and hears his fellow officers discuss his propensity for violence while Bobby defends him. He stands silent as women weep as a direct result of his philandering nature and humiliating treatment. Lastly, Zack catches a glimpse of Sandy and their son living a loving but humble existence.

The gray mist dissolves. Through the vapors,

departed family members materialize. His mother, father and brother reach out and embrace him, offering their unconditional love. Zack savors his emotional reunion. When the Angel beckons him to come forth, he loses sight of his loved ones. He hears the voice in his head saying, *It is not your time. You must return to Earth.*

Zack focuses on his ethereal guide. Confused and angry, he challenges, "You've got to be kidding! Am I in Heaven or Hell?" He pauses and scans the horizon before adding, "This must be an illusion 'cause the God I was taught to believe in wouldn't be this cruel."

Hoping for a reprieve, Zack falls to his knees and folds his hands in prayer. He weeps like a child and begs for mercy. The Angel is deeply touched by his heart wrenching appeal. She pulls the gold cord, summoning the Divine Council. Instantaneously, Zack finds himself standing beside a young boy inside the Heavenly chambers.

The gathering place is alive with shimmering lights and throbs rhythmically to the beat of one pulse. A long table appears out of nowhere with five council members seated in place. The boy stands on the left. Zack is on the right. The council members turn their heads in unison and focus on the child. All five voices become one and project, *Since you were first to arrive Jason, your voice will fill the chambers sooner than later.*

I step forward, glance around at the council members and begin, "I'm Thomas Jason Frazier. An evil man, a supposed man of God, murdered four of my friends and me. He convinced the legal authorities, our families and the religious community he was wounded trying to save us." Taking the time to look at each member of the council, I stop talking and walk the full extent of the table. I continue pleading my case, saying, "I want to end this nightmare and avenge my death as well as the deaths of all the other people he has murdered."

All five members speak to me in one breath. Curious, they ask, *How do you plan to seek revenge?*

I stand erect and don't flinch. My eyes reflect my determination as I explain, "I don't plan to kill him if that's what you're asking."

Zack interrupts, "I'd kill the son-of-a ..."

Suddenly and unexpectedly, Zack is lifted up by unseen forces and shook like a rag doll. He can't utter a sound because his jaws are clamped shut. As he thrashes about in the air, the Council members look up at him and chide, *Such language is not tolerated on this plain of existence. Hold your tongue or this meeting will cease to be.*

Zack's body stops shaking and floats down to its previous position. Dumbfounded, he takes a defensive stance but keeps his mouth shut.

Attention shifts back to me and I continue, "I want Deacon John arrested and tried for his crimes.

74

Then, our families can have closure and not feel guilty because they let us go on a camping trip." Shaking my head, I argue, "I can't stay in Heaven as long as he is free to hurt other innocent people. I just can't."

My words echo in the ethers. There is a pregnant pause before the Divine Council looks at Zack and proceeds, *Now, we will hear your argument.*

Zack straightens his posture and draws a deep breath. Teary eyed, he begins, "I'm Zachary David Lee. My life is nothing more than a black hole. Everyone I ever loved has died and left me behind. Now, I've come to Heaven only to have another door slammed in my face." Looking from one member to the next, he explains, "I don't claim to be a nice guy but I have dedicated my life to solving crimes and putting bad guys in jail. Nevertheless, I'm consumed with bitterness and live an empty existence. If my soul is forced to return to its physical body, I will be serving a life sentence for a crime I didn't commit."

The council members move as one. They spread their hands open on the table. In unison, they counter, *You have wealth, good health, high intelligence, purpose, respect and a loving aunt. What prevents you from finding happiness?*

Zack walks the length of the table, studying the unique features of each celestial counselor before moving on to the next. Finding them identical in form and demeanor, Zack answers, "Money can't buy love or happiness. I consider my body a vehicle and work hard to keep it in good condition. My intellect constantly questions my purpose. I realize my peers respect me but they don't like me. And, most women curse the day I was born." He reaches the end of the table, turns and walks back in the same manner. He explains, "My aunt loves me like a son but I can't stand to be around her. When I look at her, I remember the day my brother drowned. I hear the explosion in my head the night my mother committed suicide. .And, my fading memory of my father surfaces and causes me great pain. Please don't force me to return to my miserable existence."

The Divine Council looks at Zack and me simultaneously. The five voices explain, *Jason's body is no longer inhabitable. It is dead and buried. Zack's body is still functional. It will mend. However, if Zack's soul refuses to fight for life, his body will cease to function. Furthermore, If Jason's soul refuses to remain in this dimension and returns to haunt the earth, another soul is lost. Consequently, we have two souls and one body."*

A deafening silence prevails in the Heavenly chambers. After what seems like an eternity, the council members propose, *There is only one option. If either of you rejects this offer, Jason will remain here and Zack will return to Earth.*

Zack and I stare intently at the Divine Council, waiting for our fates to be determined. At last, the members focus on me in one unified movement and confide, *Should we allow your soul to take possession of Zack's body, you will be obligated to live and die as Zack Lee. Furthermore, you, Jason, will be responsible for his karmic debts. If and when these debts are settled, you will be granted an opportunity to pursue your own agenda.*

A hush falls over the Heavenly chambers as a caveat is attached to the bargain. The five voices reveal, *Should you break your word and attempt to kill your nemesis, you will suffer a massive heart attack and die before you can harm a hair on his head.*

Shocked and concerned, Zack interrupts, "How can you hold such a young boy bound by such an extreme condition?"

Without glancing in Zack's direction, the council members hold their focus on me and proclaim, *This is the fate of a walk-in soul.*

Looking at Zack and me simultaneously, the five voices ask, *Is this ethereal contract understood and agreed upon by each of you?*

I nod my head. Showing resistance, Zack protests, "I hate my life! More to the point, I hate myself.! But, I just can't buy into this deal! A child stands before you whose been robbed of his life by a serial killer! It is cruel and unusual punishment to ask him to run the risk of dying twice because of this homicidal maniac!"

The Divine Council looks at Zack and smiles for the first time. Nodding their heads in agreement, the voices proclaim, *This is why you are up here instead of knocking on the door of the netherworld. You're not nearly as damned as you think you are.*

After a moment of silence, the Council gets back to business and explains, *There are no children on this level of existence. Jason may look like a child but the essence of his soul is the same as your own, being an equal part of the Godhead.* Turning their attention back to me, the Council advises, *If you take possession of Zack's body, you will have no memory of this pact. You will literally pick up at the same place he left off with only one major difference. Your soul will retain its original imprint.*

Curious, Zack interrupts again and ask, "What does that mean?"

Without blinking one of their ten eyes, the five voices elaborate, *If a soul needs love for nourishment, it will draw love. If a soul thrives on hate, hate will be its reward.* Focusing on me, the council continues, *Your subconscious mind will assist in making the transition subtle rather than radical so as not to alert close friends and relative that a different soul inhabits Zack's body.*

The Council members look back at Zack and expound, *You have a different fate. You will be required to enter another level of existence, the dimension of nurture and healing. When your soul is rejuvenated, you will join your loved ones and abide in Heaven.* After a moment of reflection, the Divine Council looks at both of us at the same time and asks, *Is this ethereal process understood and agreed upon by each of you?*

I don't feel intimidated or threatened by the

conditions of the pact and exclaim, "Yes, I agree to the terms."

Suppressing his doubts, Zack states, "If Jason is willing to assume the risk; I won't stand in his way. I agree to the conditions."

The Heavenly Council disappears at the same instant Zack vanishes from sight. My guardian Angel comes forward and spreads its wings. A panoramic screening of Zack's existence on Earth is revealed. After the viewing, his mother, father and brother appear and embrace me, offering words of love and encouragement. Eleanor shares a personal message.

Suddenly and unexpectedly, my human energy field dissolves. Instantaneously, I'm hurled into a tunnel of darkness.

******

My body jolts! I gasp for air! The doctor drops his chart and it bounces off the tile floor! Everyone in the emergency room stares at me, awestruck! Askance, my eyes scan the room. The doctor is the first to regain his composure. He leans over to examine me.

I thrash about on the table and ask, "Where am I? Why am I here?"

The doctor restrains my movements and answers, "You're in the emergency room. You were in an automobile accident."

I'm suddenly aware of the injuries to my chest

and legs. Struggling to communicate with the doctor, I fight the pain and whisper, "Was anybody else involved? Were they hurt?"

The doctor smiles and responds, "The other driver received minor scrapes and bruises which required little more than a Band-Aid." He stops talking and listens to my heart beat through the earpieces of his stethoscope. Then, he continues, "I thought we'd lost you. Your lungs collapsed. You stopped breathing. I was calling the time of death when you revived and nearly scared the life out of us."

I stare directly into the doctor's eyes and ask, "How long?"

The doctor answers, "You had no pulse or heart rhythm for ... " He glances up at the clock and concludes, "about eighteen minutes."

Happy to be alive, I grin from ear to ear and joke, "Do you think my name will be mentioned in the Guinness Book of Records?"

The doctor chuckles and replies, "I don't know about the Guinness Book of Records; but I'm fairly certain you hold the record here." He turns to take a vial from his nurse as he offers, "It looks like we better get to work on you. I'm going to give you something for pain. "

As the serum reaches my bloodstream, I drift off into a deep sleep. I have dreams of Jack and my parents. I dream about Angels.

****

I awaken to find both legs in casts hoisted high in the air. I survey the room and see Aunt Ruth asleep in the chair beside my bed. She hears my movements and opens her eyes. Her demeanor reflects her concern. I catch her eye and extend my arms, beckoning for her to come closer. In a loving tone, I whisper, "Come over here and let me hug you."

Surprised but delighted by my show of affection, Ruth gets up, bends down and hugs me. Fighting back tears, she speaks in a trembling voice, "I was so afraid I was going to lose you. I couldn't bear the thought of it." She catches her breath and gasps, "I love you so much!"

Staring into her eyes, I ramble. "I dreamt I was being chased by a madman and murdered. I went to Heaven and saw Angels with crystal white wings. Words weren't spoken. Communication was telepathic." I catch my breath and elaborate, "An angel spread my whole life in front of me. It wasn't the same as watching a movie. I saw it and lived it simultaneously. I can't explain it. It's too hard to find the right words.

Ruth stands and listens to my ramblings. Noting her confusion, I exclaim, "I saw Jack and Mom and Dad! We hugged and kissed. We talked for what seemed like an eternity. We made peace ... all of us."

My aunt doesn't want to upset me by challenging

my claims. She strokes my hair as tears fill her eyes. In a condescending tone, Ruth responds, "I'm sure you did."

I see the look of disbelief in her eyes. I become more insistent and counter, "I know you don't believe me but it's true."

Ruth pats me on the shoulder and sighs. In a sad voice, she admits, "I'd really like to believe Eleanor, Eric and Jack are in Heaven together; but I can't. You know … because … " Her voice chokes and she can't finish her sentence.

I grab her hands and hold them over my heart. Trying to comfort her, I whisper, "It doesn't matter to God that Mom committed suicide. I don't mean it doesn't matter, of course, it matters. But when a person commits suicide, their soul is sent to a special place to be healed. When it's healthy again, the soul comes back to Heaven and abides therein."

Ruth pulls away from me. She scrutinizes the drip being fed into my vein and thinks it might be contributing to my delusions. In a shrill voice, she suggests, "Are you high on drugs?"

As she stands over me frowning, I gaze up at Ruth and really see her for the first time. Her stature is slim and graceful, standing five feet four inches in height. Her azure eyes are the same deep shade as mine. Combed in a short chic style, her auburn hair accentuates her flawlessly, fair complexion. I have to admit she is strikingly beautiful for a woman of fifty-four.

I see the fear in her eyes and start laughing. I giggle, "I'm not drunk. When my heart stopped, I went to Heaven. I'll prove it by telling you a secret only you and Mom share." Trying to control my exhilaration, I recall, "When you turned sixteen, grandpa bought you a new Ford Mustang. The next day, you drove mom downtown. When you went to park, you backed into a car. The two of you panicked. When you realized nobody saw the accident, you left the scene and never looked back."

As my aunt looks at me in utter amazement, I go on, "The two of you went home and didn't mention the accident. When your dad saw the dent and asked about it, you claimed you didn't know how it got there. Mom heard you lie but she didn't tattletale. Neither of you ever mentioned it again."

Ruth is startled by my revelation. She sits down on the side of my bed and clutches her chest. Barely above a whisper, she confides, "How could you possibly know that? It was a secret she took to her grave. Did she say anything else?"

I look lovingly at my aunt, smile and answer, "She loves you very much. She is grateful and proud of you for raising me." As Ruth surrenders to her emotions, I'm taken aback. In all the years I've been with her, I've never seen her cry. Trying to offer comfort, I say, "Don't cry. Mom is happy and peaceful. Her soul is at peace. She is surrounded by unconditional love."

Ruth dries her eyes and heaves a sigh of relief. She stares at me for a moment before exclaiming, "Thank God! I've lived with the fear she was burning in Hell. I prayed God would forgive her but I was so afraid He wouldn't be able to." She takes a deep breath and declares, "I don't know where you've been or what you saw; but nobody ever knew our secret. I'm just old and crazy enough to think maybe you did go to Heaven!"

I continue to smile as I drift back to sleep. My words are barely audible as I persist, "I did, Aunt Ruth. I really did."

Chapter 8

Settling Debts

I sleep through the night. When I wake up, I'm surprised to see my aunt sitting by the bed. In a puzzled voice, I ask, "What are you doing here?"

Ruth rises to her feet, walks over and stands by my bed. Immediately, she recognizes the cold, hostile look in my eyes. She backs away and hesitates before asking, "Don't you remember talking to me last night?"

I look at her with a blank stare. I don't even bother to answer.

****

Several days pass. I'm well on the road to recovery. Although my legs are in casts, my cuts and bruises are mending. While Ruth sits in a chair reading a book, I lie in bed watching television. There is a knock on the door. Bobby sticks his head inside the room and asks, "Are you up for a visit?"

Happy to see a friendly face, I smile and wave him inside. In a loud voice, I exclaim, "Come on in!" I point at Ruth and say, "I don't think you've met my aunt?"

Bobby strolls into the room and extends his arm. Ruth meets him halfway and shakes his hand. I make introductions. The two of them exchange polite conversation. While they talk, I study my partner's appearance.

Bobby is thirty-two years of age. He stands five feet ten inches. His hazel eyes twinkle with a devilish glint. His shortly cropped hair is sandy blonde. His lips are full, accenting his straight, white teeth. As he exposes a broad grin, I notice he is ruggedly handsome.

Running true to form, Bobby plays the gentleman and lies, "Zack has spoken of you often. I hate our introduction has to take place under such circumstances." Turning his attention back to me, Bobby whistles and exclaims, "Man, you're one lucky son of a gun! I saw your Porsche! I'm amazed you walked away and lived to talk about it."

I grin, point at my legs and retort, "I didn't actually walk away but I'm lucky to be alive."

Standing at the foot of my bed, Bobby glibly admits, "It would've had a difficult time breaking in a new partner."

Ruth senses we need some privacy. She grabs her purse. Making an excuse to leave, she looks at Bobby and asks, "Would you keep Zack company for a little while? I'd like to go to the cafeteria and have a good, hot cup of coffee."

Smiling, Bobby responds, 'Not a problem. Take your time." As soon as she leaves the room, he retrieves a chair, turns it to face me and sits down. Concerned, he exclaims, "Man, you really flipped out before you had your accident! What in the world was going on in your head?'

I study Bobby's face for an instant. Raising an eyebrow, I ask, "Do you really care?"

Bobby meets my gaze and answers, "If I didn't care I wouldn't ask."

I take a deep breath and exhale. I stare into Bobby's eyes and respond, "I guess the best place to start is at the beginning …"

******

Forty-five minutes later, Bobby finds Ruth sitting at a table in the cafeteria. She looks up and gestures for him to join her. He comes over and sits down. Worried, she inquires, "How did Zack seem to you?"

Shrugging his shoulders, Bobby answers, "Maybe a little worse for wear but okay in general. Why do you ask?"

Studying his features, Ruth inquires, "How well

do you really know Zack?"

Bobby glances away for a brief moment, turns back, makes eye contact with Ruth and answers, "To be perfectly honest, I only know him on a professional level." He chuckles and adds, "He'd never win the title of Mr. Congeniality; but he's a damn good detective."

Trusting her instincts, Ruth confides, "I don't mean to burden you with my problems but I need to talk to someone." She takes a deep breath and confides, "Zack goes through the motions of living but he hasn't loved anybody or anything since his brother and parents died. He isn't cruel or sadistic but he never shows any emotion." She hesitates for a moment before asking, "Do you understand what I'm trying to say?

Bobby shuffles uncomfortably in his chair and admits, "I don't know what you want me to say?"

Trying to gain his confidence, Ruth smiles sweetly and elaborates, "Since his accident, Zack has exhibited schizophrenic tendencies. One minute, he's the cold and indifferent nephew I've always known. The next minute, he's this kind and gentle man I don't even recognize."

Bobby rationalizes, "He survived a deadly accident. He's on a lot of drugs and his system isn't used to them." He stops talking, takes a deep breath and offers, "When the doctor weans him off the pain medication, I'm sure his disorientation will pass and he'll be back to normal in no time."

Ignoring his reassurance, Ruth confides, "He wakes up all hours of the day and night, screaming in fear. He thinks someone is trying to kill him. When I ask him about his paranoia, he refuses to discuss it. Quite frankly, I'm thinking about consulting a psychiatrist."

Bobby has a blank expression on his face and doesn't respond. Ruth taps her cup with her spoon to get his undivided attention. Then, she pries, "How did he seem to you? What did he talk about?"

Bobby glances at the other people in the cafeteria before he focuses on Ruth. He speaks very low, saying, "He told me about his past. Then, he spoke about my personal life, telling me secrets I never told anyone, including my wife. And, he talked about seeing and hearing spirits when he was in the dead zone."

Wide-eyed, Ruth exclaims, "How does he know those things?"

Bobby shifts his weight and confesses, "I don't know. I do know he was legally dead for more than fifteen minutes and he's lucky to be alive. Beyond that, I haven't got a clue."

Ruth puts her elbows on the table and leans on them Looking physically and emotionally exhausted, she asks, "What do you think I should do?"

Needing time to think. Bobby signals for time out. He gets up, walks over to the food bar and pours two cups of steaming coffee. After he pays the clerk, Bobby returns to the table. He puts one cup in front of Ruth and holds onto the other. He sits down, takes a couple of sips and answers, "All you can do is give him time to heal, mentally and physically."

Ruth drinks some coffee, smiles at Bobby and agrees, "That's all I can do, isn't it?" She takes another swig and inquires, "What about you? What are you going to do?"

Bobby leans back in his chair. Although he appears to be answering Ruth, he is actually talking to himself. His eyes twinkle as he answers, "Zack plans to open a private detective agency in Atlanta when he is up and running again. He offered me a partnership." Bobby lets his chair drop to the floor as he finishes, "I'm going to keep my job until he's ready to make his move. Then, I'm going to quit and go with him."

******

Two weeks before Christmas, Ruth makes arrangements for me to be moved into her home. She transforms one of the massive bedrooms into a makeshift ward. With my uncle's blessings, Ruth plays the role of nurse and takes control of my healing process. While my body mends, we spend hours of quality time together. After years of running away from love, I finally allow myself to learn the true meaning of Christmas and family unity.

I stay with Ruth and Paul until late February. Except for needing crutches to walk, my recover is complete. I'm anxious to get home. Samson and Delilah have been in the care of the gardener and grieving over my absence. When I limp into the house, both dogs sense a subliminal difference in me but are delighted to offer their unconditional love.

******

In early April, I drop by the Von Haven home unannounced. Richard answers the door. He looks at me and backs up. The shock on his face diminishes as he notices my physical disability.

I meet his gaze and begin, "Mr. Von Haven, I'm sorry to come unannounced but I figured you would refuse to see me if I called first."

Richard's eyes blaze with anger. Waiting for me to make a threatening move, he balls his fists. In a high-pitched voice, he retorts, "You got that right! You've got your nerve coming here!"

Propping my crutches beside me, I lean back against the railing. In a meek voice, I confide, "I was compelled to come and clear the air."

Richard laughs out loud. Through clenched teeth, he snarls, "What about! The satisfaction you derive from solving murder cases at other people's expense?"

My posture stiffens. I grab my crutches, place them under my arms and put my weight on them. I raise my voice and retort, "I didn't turn your world upside down! Your wife did!"

Richard looks askance and declares, "I must be confused! You said you came to clear the air not stir up more shit!"

His remark reminds me of my purpose. I apologize by saying, "I admit I lost control when I worked on Mitzi's case. But when I saw your daughter's body, lying on the shore, drowned and abandoned, my past overwhelmed me."

Befuddled, Richard takes a step backward and exclaims, "What in the Hell are you talking about?"

Shifting my weight, I lean on my crutches. Using my hands to make my point, I confide, "To make a long story short, my twin brother drowned when he was Mitzi's age. Although his death was ruled an accident, my mother was to blame."

Richard is caught off guard by my startling revelation. He can't think of a comeback and stands speechless. As pangs of sorrow and curiosity overwhelm him, Richard gasps, "That's awful! What happened to your mother?"

I fight back tears and confide, "She couldn't live with her guilt. She committed suicide. "

Richard relaxes his stance. The muscles in his face quit twitching. Without saying another word, he stands and stares at me. His silence indicates that some degree of understanding exists between us. I put my full weight on my crutches and slowly descend the stairs. Talking over my shoulder, I offer, "I apologize for intruding on your privacy. I know my visit is totally inappropriate but something compelled me to come. I can't explain it but I needed to say I'm sorry about everything."

Richard leans over the railing and looks down. He sees the cab waiting below. He watches me struggle to open the door. Smiling half-heartedly for the first time since our meeting, he hollers, "It took guts to come here especially in the shape you're in! You got balls! I'll give you that much!"

I toss my crutches into the backseat and wave before disappearing inside the car. Richard watches the vehicle back out of the driveway and vanishes from sight. He walks back inside the house and closes the door behind him.

******

Several months later, I sit in a coffee shop, facing the door. Vicky enters, glances in my direction, hesitates momentarily before walking over to the table. Shielding a black eye, the strikingly beautiful woman refuses to meet my gaze. I remain sitting but pull out a chair. Vicky sits down.

I begin the conversation by saying, "Thanks for coming. I was afraid you wouldn't show."

Vicky unfolds her napkin and places it in her lap.

She scans the room looking for the waitress. Nervous and uncomfortable, she replies, "I started not to but my curiosity got the best of me."

I watch her fidgeting and wait to get her undivided attention. When she finally makes eye contact, I say, "I want to apologize for my inexcusable behavior. I know you are a decent woman … "

Vicky's anger surfaces and she interrupts, " I'm not looking for compliments. I'm here for curiosity's sake; so, get to the chase."

Talking in a soothing tone, I try to dust her emotional feathers by saying, "You are a beautiful and intelligent woman … "

Waving her finger in front of my nose, Vicky shakes her head. For a second time, she counters, "The Zack I know makes a habit of preying on vulnerable women. He offers words of comfort long enough to put his plan in motion. And, that plan is getting laid. Since we both know that ain't gonna happen, what is today's Modus Operandi?"

I hold my arms up in surrender and admit, "Your insight regarding my character is phenomenal. I don't deny my bad reputation 'cause I've earned it. But, when was the last time you looked in the mirror?"

Vicky looks down as the waitress approaches the table to take our order. I order coffee for the both of us. Waiting for our drinks, we sit in silence. After the cups are on the table and the waitress has moved out of hearing distance. She sighs deeply before admitting, "That's been my main order of business lately. I know Jim loves me but he blames me for everything that goes wrong in his life. I can't continue to be his punching bag." As tears roll down her cheeks, she wipes them away with her hand and gasps, "I've made up my mind to leave him. If he misses me, maybe he'll get some counseling. If that happens, I'll give him another chance. Otherwise, I'm history."

I get a cramp in my right leg, lean over and massage my calf. Looking up, I ask, "What are you waiting for?"

Vicky takes a sip of coffee and straightens her posture. Avoiding my eyes, she answers, "It takes money to start a new life."

I pull my checkbook out of my pocket, rip out a check and start endorsing it. Without looking up, I ask, "How much money will it take to move and get settled? Give yourself some leeway for finding a decent job."

Vicky becomes flustered and embarrassed. She glances around the room as though someone is playing a trick on her. She looks back at me with her eyes open wide. Gulping for air, she confesses, "I'd love to have the pride to turn down your offer. But, I'm afraid if I don't leave now I'll lose my nerve." Grabbing a figure out of the air, Vicky stutters, "Five thousand dollars should be more than sufficient."

I write down that amount and continue filling out the check. Vicky is stunned by my generosity and feels an explanation is in order. She questions, "Why are you doing this? I'm not your responsibility. I need to know why you're helping me."

I stop writing, look up and respond, "I've lashed out at people who weren't responsible for my pain all my life. Now, I need to atone for my action. So, I'm not helping you so much as I'm helping myself." I pause a moment and then add, "My karmic debts have to be paid before I can get on with my life."

Vicky leans back in her seat and stares at me. She watches me sign the check and takes it when I hand it to her. Looking embarrassed, she gasps, "I don't know what to say. I'm speechless."

I get up and take my cane off the back of the chair. For the first time, Vicky notices I'm physically impaired. She starts to comment but I put my finger to my mouth indicating words aren't necessary. As we walk toward the exit, Vicky stuffs the check into her purse. When we reach the door, she pecks me on the cheek, turns and walks away.

Chapter 9

Letting Go

I send Bobby ahead to Atlanta to set up our detective agency. While he gets licensed, finds office space and hires employees, I have one more issue to resolve. On Sunday, June 21, 1998, I climb into my new Cadillac, take the interstate and drive toward Florida's west coast. I'm determined to resolve my issues with Sandy and my son.

Monday morning, June 22nd, I stroll into a diner located on the outskirts of Tampa. I sit down at a table near the rear of the café. As the waitress approaches, I look up and smile. Holding her pad and pencil in a writing position, the young woman stands and waits for my order.

I study the server's features. Standing five feet six inches in statue, Sandy is much slimmer than I remember. Her streaked blonde hair is messy and haphazardly stuffed beneath a striped scarf matching her red and white, wrinkled uniform. Her lips are painted red. Her smile is forced. Distracting from her clear complexion, worry lines and tiny crow's feet define her face. Her hazel eyes cast a hint that life has become a fight for survival.

Glancing at her customer, Sandy is startled to recognize me and exclaims, "Are you Zack Lee?"

Flattered at being identified, I smile broadly and respond, "Yes, I am! And, you're the beautiful cheerleader who rooted our team to victory."

Sandy's smile vanishes. She puts her hands on her hips and glares at me. Insulted, she retorts, "I did a lot more than cheer for you."

Embarrassed by my left-handed compliment, I glance away. After an uncomfortable silence, I look up at her and admit, "I didn't mean my remark as an insult. When I saw you, I remembered how we met. You were a real ball of fire."

Sandy frowns and blows her bangs out of her eyes. She quips, "If you look at me now, you'll see that energy has just about fizzled out." She raises her pen and asks, "What would you like to drink?"

I order, "Coffee ... and a glass of water, please."

I watch Sandy walk back to the counter. I continue to observe while she carries trays of food out to her other customers. I'm saddened by her hostile attitude and low opinion of herself.

Sandy returns with my coffee and slams it down on the table. On the defensive, I counter, "I didn't come to start another war. I came to make peace. And, I'm willing to make restitution. But, I'm not going to discuss it here. Name a time and place."

Taking a moment to think, Sandy replies, "My shift ends in fifteen minutes. Meet me at the restaurant across the street."

Sandy leaves and continues waiting on her patrons. I down my coffee, lay five dollars on the table and leave the crowded diner. I go directly across the street and disappear inside the restaurant. Twenty minutes later, Sandy enters the eating establishment. I meet her at the door and guide her to a secluded booth in the rear of the building. As we take our seats, Sandy is quiet and reserved. I catch her eye and begin, "We have some unfinished business to discuss."

Uncomfortable and resentful, Sandy shifts her position. She retaliates, "I don't think we have anything to discuss. We had a high school fling. It ended badly. We went our separate ways."

Dumbfounded, I ask, "What about the child?"

Sandy lashes out, "To the best of my recollection, you suggested I get an abortion!" A hush fills our space. We sit glaring at each other. Finally, Sandy heaves a deep sigh and reports, "The child to whom you're referring is our son, Jack. Everybody calls him, Jay."

Tears well in my eyes as a lump forms in my throat. Sandy watches my reaction and is surprised to see me show emotion. She changes the subject by asking, "What have you been doing since graduation?"

In robotic fashion, I report, "I went to Florida State for a couple of years. I dropped out and went to work for the police in Jacksonville. Not to sound egotistical, I'm a damn good detective." I pause before going on, "I live in a big house overlooking the St. Johns River. My only companions are my Dobermans, Samson and Delilah."

Sandy laughs out loud and giggles, "Now, that's apropos. You always had a Samson complex, afraid everybody was out to get you." She quits laughing and pries, "Is that all you have to say for yourself?"

Wanting to be open and honest, I confide, "I was involved in a serious car accident about eight months ago. I literally died for eighteen minutes." I stop talking, take a deep breath and elaborate, "For lack of a better explanation, I was born again into the same body. Since then, every aspect of my life has changed."

As she listens, Sandy studies my features. She recalls a good-looking kid. Now, she is gazing at a mature and extremely handsome man with a strong, muscular physique. But, Sandy is not looking at me with adoring eyes. She has long since realized our attraction was puppy love. She is looking at the father of her child. Gazing into my eyes, Sandy remarks, "I remember you had blue eyes but I don't remember them being such a deep shade. They are absolutely mesmerizing."

I am momentarily distracted by her observation and comment, "That's funny. My aunt said the same thing. They look the same to me. I can't explain it."

Looking away, Sandy admits, "I was devastated when you rejected me and our baby. I spent years hating you. I cursed your name more times than I can count." She stops, takes a deep breath and blurts out, "I was so embarrassed by the fact I was pregnant and not married, I told everyone you were killed in an automobile accident!"

Shocked by her statement, I counter, "My son thinks I'm dead?"

Sandy doesn't blink or flinch. She confesses, "Yes, I didn't want him to know his father didn't want him. And, I didn't want him to think I was promiscuous. I felt my explanation would suffice."

Astonished, I gasp for air and clutch my chest! Speechless, I sit and stare at Sandy. When I finally get my voice back, I reveal, "I'm here to fulfill my moral and financial obligation to both of you. I ask only one thing in return. I want to have a relationship with my son."

Sandy looks shocked. She shifts in her seat as she gasps for air. Not wanting to deal with the past, she shuts down. Then, out of the blue, Sandy recalls, "Didn't you have a brother who died? Wasn't he your twin?!" Waiting for my reaction, Sandy holds her breath. Needing to breathe, she nudges me and exclaims, "You could pretend to be him! What do you think?"

I laugh heartily and retort, "That's the dumbest idea I ever heard." After I stop laughing, I counter, "Even if it worked what purpose would it serve?"

Sandy responds, "You could have a loving relationship with your son. Jay could have a father figure. And, I wouldn't be caught in a big, fat lie!"

I take Sandy's hand in mine and look into her eyes. I reason, "What is the point of solving one problem by creating a bigger one? Besides, I can't assume a dead man's identity even if I wanted to." Sandy jerks her hand away and refuses to look at me. In a low voice, I admit, "If I was the old Zack, I'd stoop to any level to get my way; but I'm not."

Tearing up, Sandy stares into space. I take hold of her chin and turn her head in my direction. I explain, "When I was fighting for my life, I swore to God I'd change if I had another chance. I promised I'd stop being vindictive, lying to everybody and hurting people who cared about me. More to the point, I vowed to quit hating myself." Speaking to her soul, I question, "If I don't hold up my end of the bargain, what was the point in coming back from the dead?"

Exacerbated, Sandy retorts, "Are you asking me or telling me?"

I refuse to dignify her question with an answer. Giving her a chance to accept the radical difference in my character, I remain quiet and subdued. Slowly, it dawns on Sandy that her moment of truth has arrived. Heaving an audible sigh, she agrees, "You're right. It's time for us to take responsibility for our actions. But, I can't make a decision in a matter of minutes. And, I want to discuss it with my fiancé."

Shifting my position in the booth, I nod and say, "I know you raised Jay alone. And, I would never do anything to hurt your relationship. But if you allow me to share in his rearing, I'll guarantee you financial security."

Insulted, Sandy jerks her hand away. As her temper flares, she retaliates, "Are you trying to buy your way into his life?"

Not backing down, I counter, "No, but you should know by now life isn't fair. Sometimes, you have to give in order to take. And, I have no intention of being an anonymous benefactor."

Sandy looks at her watch, picks up her purse and rises to leave. She looks down at me and instructs, "Give me the name and number where you're staying. I'll get back to you with my decision."

I reach for my business card and jot the information down. I hand it to Sandy and get up.

Standing, I report, "I'll be here for the rest of the week. Call me anytime."

Sandy has managed to control her personal feelings. Suddenly and unexpectedly, a flood of emotions overwhelms her. She plops back down in her seat and cries hysterically. As she sobs, Sandy gasps, "I loved you so much. I dreamt about the life we'd share. But, my obsession with you was as wrong as your rejection of me. We were both too young to know what we were doing."

I sit down and pull Sandy into my arms. As I embrace her, tears fill my eyes and run down my cheeks. As the ghosts of the past dance in the shadows, my only solace is the realization that I'm finally facing my demons.

******

Later in the evening, I sit alone in a motel room and read the local paper. The telephone rings and breaks the silence. I answer, "Hello, this is Zack."

Sandy says, "I hope I'm not interrupting?"

Grimacing, I reply, "No problem, I'm glad you called."

Sandy reports, "I've given a great deal of thought to our conversation. I talked to Gary." There is a slight pause before she continues, "He agrees with you. He thinks it is time to be honest with Jay."

Excited to be getting a second chance, I ask,

"What's the plan?"

Sandy answers, "We want you to come over tomorrow night at eight. Then, we'll tell our son the truth."

Although my voice chokes, I manage to say, "I'll see you then."

******

Gary and I sit on the couch while Sandy paces the floor and glances at us for support. Gathering her courage, she calls Jay. After a few moments, the young boy slides down the banister, runs into the room and stops in his tracks. Seeing the somber expressions on our faces, the youngster senses bad news. His high spirits plummet.

Jay is four feet seven inches in height and average weight. Partially due to tone and Tampa sunshine, his skin is tan. His hair is the same dark hue as mine. His eyes are blue and clearly defined by long dark eyelashes. His lips are full concealing uneven teeth. When he smiles, Jay's dimples become his prominent feature.

I'm mesmerized by his uncanny resemblance to Jack. Overwhelmed by the similarity, my mind goes blank. In a matter of seconds, the sound of Sandy's voice brings me out of my reverie. Consciously pushing my memories back into yesterday, I focus on the moment and take my turn explaining to Jay why he is meeting me for the first time.

Looking from one adult to the other, Jay listens

attentively. Being young and open-minded, he accepts the news with resilience. He is not upset, hurt or angry. Amazingly, he is happy and excited about have a "real" dad. Grinning from ear to ear, my son walks over to me and throws his arms around my neck. Overcome with emotion, tears roll down my cheeks.

I remain in Tampa for three more weeks. I take Jay to the nearby amusement parks, including Disney World. We go to several little league games and I instruct him on the finer points of hitting a baseball. We enjoy sun and fun on the beach. On one occasion, Sandy and Gary join us on a picnic. Each of us soaks in the beautiful climate, peaceful setting and newfound love. Finally, the time comes for me to resume my life.

Shortly before I leave, I inform Sandy of the details regarding their new finances. Needing to express her independence, Sandy asks, "What if I don't want to move to Jacksonville?"

I answer, "You don't have to live in my house. You can sell it and buy a home anywhere you choose." I take a deep breath and continue, "I don't want to lord over you and Jay. I simply want to improve the quality of your lives."

Jay bounds down the stairs, runs into the room and interrupts our conversation. I wink at Sandy and hand him my car keys. I look down at my son and lie, "I left my briefcase in the car. Will you get it for me?"

Jay grins, takes the keys and rushes outside. Sandy and I walk to the porch and watch as he reaches the car. He opens the door and a golden Lab jumps out. Jay laughs and leans down to pet the puppy. As the dog licks him in the face, he giggles, looks up at us and hollers, "Is this puppy for me?"

I yell, "Yep, he's all yours!"

******

The following morning, I head home to put my affairs in order. I visit Aunt Ruth and bring her up to speed on Sandy and Jay. I inform her of the financial arrangements. She is delighted by my newfound sense of responsibility and offers to check on them regularly.

With a clear conscience, I depart for my new life in Atlanta on Friday. I arrive in the city early in the evening. Bobby meets me at the hotel. We enjoy a robust dinner. Tired from the long drive, I call it a night. Before going our separate ways, we schedule a meeting for the following morning.

Early Saturday morning, Bobby and I meet in the hotel lobby. He drives me to a nearby condominium and waits for me to inspect the living accommodations. After touring the two-story brick town home, I exclaim, "This is first class! I like it!"

We leave the complex and head to the office. Our space occupies the entire top level of a brick commercial building and displays many windows overlooking the courtyard. The interior is sectioned off into a lobby, three small offices, two oversized offices and a lounge. The furnishings consist of leather couches and chairs, tables, lamps and wall hangings depicting different breeds of hunting dogs. The accessories are tiffany style with accent shades of blue and burgundy. A huge oil painting of two bloodhounds hangs on the wall behind my desk, adding a hint of ambiance to our joint enterprise.

I'm pleased with Bobby's ability to select and decorate the office. After offering words of praise, I inquire, "Tell me about the detectives you've hired?"

Bobby begins, "The eldest member is Sam Brooks. He is recently retired from the Atlanta Police Department. He has a good rapport with his former cohorts, which might come in handy from time to time."

I respond, "Sounds like an excellent choice. Who's next?"

Bobby answers, "Rick Mason is an ex-Marine who served as an 'MP.' He didn't reenlist 'cause of his dad's poor health. Due to his extensive travels, he's fluent in Spanish and French."

Satisfied with this recruit, I exclaim, "Sounds good. Tell me about the third man?"

Bobby replies, "Jim Zimmerman is our Oglethorpe man. He's working on his law degree and needs money to pay his tuition. He's one of the smartest men I've ever met. If he can't solve a problem, he won't quit digging until he comes up with a solution."

Impressed with Bobby's ingenuity, I feel better about my decision to relocate to Atlanta and form a business partnership. I'm consciously aware that a new business needs time to grow. And, I'm financially prepared to outlast the lean years and look forward to the good ones.

******

Nearly five years have passed since I moved to Atlanta. The five of us detectives enjoy a good working relationship. Each one of us specializes in a different area. Sam handles the messy details of divorce. Rick works with foreign clients. Jim tends to insurance matters. Bobby and I focus on missing persons and unsolved cases. Sometimes, we work together. Other times, we work alone.

The day is Thursday, May 8, 2003. I'm five months shy of my thirty-third birthday. I recline in my leather desk chair, mulling over my recent accomplishments. I live alone in a large home overlooking the Chattahoochee River. Samson and Delilah are enjoying their golden years in my care. Although a lasting and loving relationship with a woman doesn't exist, the love I share with my son gives meaning and purpose to my life.

I pick up a letter from Sandy and look at pictures of Jay. I hear a knock on the door. Bobby sticks his head through the opening and announces, "There are two ladies in the lobby. One of them has a son who went missing. I'd like for us to interview them together."

Chapter 10

Serendipity

I nod my head. Bobby disappears. I put my letter away. Bobby walks back in the room, leading two women. Instinctively, I assess each woman by her appearance. I focus on the older one first. She is a plain woman possessing no outstanding features. She has auburn hair, brown eyes and a freckled complexion. Her clothes appear to be inexpensive and hang loosely on her frail body. Looking older than her years, the lines on her face indicate life has been harsh.

I turn my head and concentrate on the younger woman, who appears to be about twenty-seven or eight. She is in stark contrast to her companion. She stands five feet two inches weighing barely one hundred pounds. Bleached tresses highlight her thick golden blonde hair. Gracefully arched brows bring attention to her almond shaped blue eyes, accentuated by thick black eyelashes. Her complexion is flawlessly fair and her lightly painted lips are full and sensual. Her dazzling smile exposes her straight white teeth. Her pretty facial features are enhanced by an hourglass figure. Stylish clothes cling to her petite form as though custom designed to remind men of the difference between the sexes. Unbeknownst to me, her physical beauty is only a prelude to her wit, charm and passion.

Bobby clears his throat to get my attention. As the two women sit down, he introduces, "Maggie Harlow, Betsy Bond, this is my partner, Zack Lee."

Stifling my attraction to Maggie, I begin, "Bobby tells me one of you has a missing child." Looking askance, I inquire, "Which one?"

Betsy holds up her hand like a child in a classroom, beckoning for attention. She answers, "Me. My son, Billy, has been missing for almost four years."

Making eye contact with Betsy, I state, "Before discussing the details, I'd like to ask a few preliminary questions." I pause before inquiring, "What brought you to our agency?"

Maggie answers, "I did."

I turn to look at her. Suddenly, I'm overcome with feelings of déjà vu. Staring, I pry, "Pardon me for asking but have we met before?"

Flattered and intrigued, Maggie smiles and answers, "I don't think so. Why do you ask?"

I continue to stare at the beautiful woman. Concentrating on her features, I try to make contact with my memory bank. Slowly, I report, "I'm not sure.

You just look familiar." Trying not to come across as a moonstruck teenager, I get back on track by inquiring, "What is your relationship with Ms. Bond?"

Focusing on the business at hand, Maggie explains, "Our relationship is based on mutual losses. A friend of mine was murdered in the mountains close to where Billy went missing. They were both in the care of the same churchman at the time of their mishaps." She stops to catch her breath before continuing, "Betsy has tried to cooperate with the police in Asheville. But, those backwoods hillbillies with badges have classified Billy as a runaway. They've made no attempt to find him. ... Billy loved his mother. He would never have run away and abandoned her."

Betsy leans forward in her seat and interjects, "Maggie has been after me to hire a private investigator. I refused 'cause I was waiting for my boy to come home." Beginning to tear up, she continues, "Now, I'm running out of time and hope."

Bobby walks over to the window and glances outside. He turns to face Betsy and asks, "Why are you so sure Billy didn't run away?

Making eye contact, Betsy straightens her posture and explains, "Billy was the man of the house. He took pride in that role. He swore he would never be like his father and abandon me." Experiencing shortness of breath, Betsy stops talking. She coughs and inhales deeply before continuing, "I met his dad when I was a barmaid. We got involved. After a few months, he admitted he was married. I know I should have told him to hit the road. But, I was young, dumb and very poor. It made me feel good for a man to tell me I was pretty and buy me presents. When I found out I was pregnant, I told him He denied responsibility. He left town in the middle of the night. I never saw or heard from him again."

Bobby inquires, "What's his name?"

Betsy replies, "Claude Daniel Higgins."

Postulating, I suggest, "Do you think there is any chance Claude might have had a change of heart, returned to Asheville and taken Billy against his will?"

Speaking for Betsy, Maggie answers, "We considered that possibility. I went to the bar Claude frequented. After some friendly persuasion, I convinced the owner to let me check his credit card receipts. I followed the paper trail and discovered Claude was killed in a car accident five years earlier."

Anxious to speak her mind, Betsy interjects, "The local police didn't even bother to follow up on Claude. They had already decided Billy left of his own accord."

I lean back in my chair and drum my fingers on the armrest. I look at Betsy and inquire, "What was your son's attitude before he went missing?"

Betsy thinks for a moment before answering, "Billy was a loner. We were dirt poor and all the kids knew it, seeing his second-hand clothes and all. He was small for his age and bullied by a few of the bigger boys. " Betsy pauses as she concentrates on his frame of mind. Then, she continues, "A group of church folk came by the house several months before he went missing. One of the deacons took a liking to Billy and invited him to join his Bible class. He told Billy they had special outings, movies, parties and so on. I felt like the church offered Billy a chance to learn about religion and make new friends. So, I pushed him into joining."

Curious, I question, "Did the church affiliation help Billy?"

Thinking before she answers, Betsy responds, "It did at first. But in no time at all, he didn't want to go back. When I asked him why, he wouldn't tell me?"

I lean forward in my chair and probe, "Did his personal habits change?"

Again, Betsy takes time to think before answering, "Billy was always open and honest with me. He didn't know how to keep a secret. A few weeks before he went missing, he became withdrawn. He didn't want to talk about anything anymore. He just wanted to stay in his room, alone."

Bobby pries, "Do you think it's possible he was drinking or using drugs?"

When drugs are mentioned, Betsy doesn't flinch. She meets Bobby head on with her answer, saying, "Not a chance! If anybody on Earth could spot an alcoholic or drug addict, it would be me 'cause I've been down that road myself. I warned Billy repeatedly about the down side of addiction. As a matter of fact, Billy got a few black eyes protecting younger kids in the neighborhood from drug dealers."

No one moves or speaks for a few moments. Betsy clears her throat before sharing, "I know my Billy. Our life wasn't perfect but he wanted to work and help improve our living conditions. He might have been having some kind of personal crisis, but he would never abandon me. I know in my heart and soul something is very, very wrong. That's why he hasn't come home."

I pull a pad out of my desk drawer, pick up a pen and start taking notes. I look up at Betsy and ask, "When and where was the last time you saw Billy?"

Noting my heightened interest, Betsy quickly responds, "I got home from work about five forty five on the evening of July 14, 1999. The deacon had left a message on the recorder. He was taking the boys to the movies after Bible study. He wanted Billy at the church by six. I got him there about five minutes late. He never came home."

Bobby walks over and sits down beside Betsy. He asks, "Who was the last person to see Billy?"

Confused, Betsy replies, "I'm not sure. Nobody ever told me."

I sit upright in my chair. Turning my attention to

Maggie, I question, "Tell me specifically how you got involved?"

Maggie responds, "As I mentioned earlier, Jason Frazier was my childhood sweetheart. He was murdered three months after he moved to Asheville. No one was ever charged for the crime and I never got over it."

I probe, "What makes you think his murder is connected to Billy's disappearance?"

Maggie doesn't blink as she answers, "Jason joined a fellowship group headed by Deacon John, the same churchman who led Billy's class." She stops talking, takes a deep breath and exhales. Her voice trembles as she continues, "In August of 1987, this man took Jason and four other boys on an overnight camping trip. During the night, all the boys were stabbed to death. Deacon John was the only member of the group to walk out of the woods alive."

Sympathetic to Maggie's loss, Bobby shakes his head. Taking over the interrogation, he confirms, "And the murderer was never caught?"

Looking through Bobby, Maggie stares into space. Without blinking, she answers, "No, his murder remains an unsolved mystery."

I'm becoming more curious with each word. I look at Maggie and inquire, "How did you meet Betsy?"

Getting frustrated by all the questions, Maggie sighs before she confides, "I'm a journalist. After

Jason's murder, I followed news reports of murdered and missing children in western North Carolina. When I read of Billy's disappearance, I became suspicious when I saw Deacon John was involved." She gets up, walks over to the window and looks outside. As she gazes down on the courtyard, she continues, "I don't believe in coincidence. I went to Asheville and found Betsy. We decided to hire a private investigator. I was drawn to your ad because it says you deal in unsolved mysteries."

Bobby poses the next question, putting emphasis on one word. He asks, "What do YOU hope to accomplish by hiring us?"

Maggie makes eye contact with Bobby and states, "I want you to investigate Billy's disappearance. If you discover any evidence about Jason's murder in the process, that's great. If not, that's fine too." She pauses, turns to look at me and finishes, "My primary concern is Billy."

I sense Maggie has her own agenda. Hoping to force her hand, I pry, "What is your role in this investigation?"

Making a grand gesture of swinging her hips provocatively, Maggie returns to her chair. She sits down and smiles demurely at me. She stops talking in her normal manner and assumes a southern drawl. Speaking slowly and prolonging her words, she says, "I simply want to provide background information and document your findings." After an uncomfortable silence, Maggie resumes her normal accent and inquires, "Does that create a problem for you boys?"

Accepting her challenge, I retort, "Not at all. If you want to play reporter, that's fine with us."

Having no intention of getting caught in the middle of the cat and mouse game Maggie and I are playing, Bobby remains quiet. Shaking his head, his eyes twinkle with amusement. I control my urge to laugh. Maggie is livid! Her nostrils flare as her eyes blaze with anger. She fights to control her temper. Everyone waits for someone else to speak. Finally, Maggie breaks the silence by stating, "I don't consider it play. It's my chosen profession."

Thinking the time is right to end the conference, I rise to my feet. I smile at both women, extend my arm and shake their hands. The women get up and walk toward the door. When they reach the doorway, I call out, "If you'll give Bobby and me a few moments to confer, I'll give you our decision."

As soon as they walk into the hallway and close the door, Bobby looks quizzically at me. Oblivious to his gaze, I mumble, "Maggie looks incredibly familiar. I can't remember where I've seen her but her face haunts me." Talking to myself, I say, "I need to make reservations at a motel in Asheville for Monday night."

Bobby is caught off guard that I have made my decision without discussing it with him. He quips, "I guess you've just answered the question as to which one of us is going to investigate this case?"

Distracted by my own thoughts, I don't look up as I reply, "I guess I have."

Chapter 11

The Scent

Early Monday morning, May 12th, I stop by the office and pick up the paperwork dealing with Billy. Numerous photographs are bunched together along with personal information, such as date of birth, height, weight, birthmarks, schoolmates and last known sighting. After discussing my itinerary with Bobby, I leave and head northeast in the direction of Asheville, North Carolina. I arrive at my destination early in the afternoon. After familiarizing myself with the main thoroughfare in the city, I check into a motel.

******

Tuesday morning, May 13th, I start my investigation at the last place Betsy saw Billy, the church. I walk into the main sanctuary and search for the pastor. I find him in the chapel and flash my credentials. We sit down in the nearest pew.

Having no distinguishing features other than a full crop of white hair and faded blue eyes, Pastor Brown is average looking for a man in his late sixties.

His ordinary appearance is overshadowed by his exaggerated sense of importance. Possessing a pious disposition, he considers himself flawless in character and design.

I begin my interrogation by identifying my purpose. I open, "I'm Zack Lee. I'm working as a private investigator on behalf of Betsy Bond. She has hired me to probe into the disappearance of her son, Billy." I pause and wait for a response. Hearing none, I go on, "Were you the minister here when Billy went missing?"

The pastor leans back and looks at me. He smiles serenely and answers, "I'm Pastor Brown. Yes, I've been the minister at this church for nearly thirty years."

I counter, "Did you know the boy?"

Pastor Brown replies, "Not really. I saw him in the church on several occasions but I don't think I spoke more than a few words to him."

Entering the building from the rear and slamming the door in the process, a female church member startles me. The pastor ignores her. I provide more details as I state, "Billy's mother informed me he was attending a study class on Wednesday nights." I get no response. I pose my next question, asking, "Do you know who was teaching the class during that time frame?"

Pastor Brown tilts his head upwards and stares at

the ceiling. Then, he asks, "How old was the boy?"

I answer, "He was thirteen."

Pastor Brown turns his head and looks toward the altar. He thinks for a few seconds before responding, "It must've been Deacon John. He teaches the class for boys between eleven and thirteen."

I make eye contact with the pastor and inquire, "What's his surname?"

Pastor Brown looks away to avoid my eyes. In a boastful tone, he confides, "His surname is Powers, John Wesley Powers to be precise."

Curious, I ask, "How long has John been a member of the church?"

Without needing time to think, the pastor answers, "He joined the church a few years after I took over the ministry, must've been the mid 70s."

I question, "Does he have family here?"

Pastor Brown replies, "No, John is an orphan."

I inquire, "What brought him to Asheville?"

Pastor Brown leans back in the pew and stares into space for a few moments. Then, he answers, "Lone Wolf."

Puzzled, I pry, "Who or what is Lone Wolf?"

Smiling as he scans the sanctuary, Pastor Brown replies, "Lone Wolf is a native American Indian. He was a member of this congregation until he graduated from high school and joined the Army. He was one of the last soldiers stationed in Vietnam." Noting my heightened interest, he elaborates, "Lone Wolf met John while they were stationed there. They took a shine to each other. Since neither of 'em had any family, they became 'blood brothers.'"

Before I have a chance to interrupt his reverie, the pastor continues, " Lone Wolf finished his tour of duty about six months before John. When he got out of the service, John followed him to Asheville. They pooled their resources and bought some property in the mountains. A few months later, they went into business together."

Eager to learn more, I ask, "What kind of business?"

Pastor Brown responds, "Arts and Crafts! Lone Wolf taught John how to carve wood by hand to make art objects and decorative furniture."

Needing more specifics, I pry, "What is Lone Wolf's full name?"

Shaking his head, Pastor Brown reports, "Don't know; never asked."

Ready to delve into the essence of the man, I inquire, "May I ask about John's character?"

Laughing lightly, Pastor Brown jokes, "You can ask but it doesn't mean you're gonna get an answer." After a pregnant pause, the pastor giggles, "I was just making you earn your money!"

The pastor and I sit silent for a few moments as he appears to be contemplating his answer. Then, he states, "John is a true man of God. He loves spreading the gospel. He offers a helping hand to the underprivileged. And, he volunteers at the YMCA counseling runaway boys." The pastor catches his breath before adding, "Matter of fact, John is a local celebrity of sorts!

My curiosity piques and I quip, "Really? Why?"

For the first time, Pastor Brown tilts his body in my direction. He smiles broadly and proudly recalls, "About sixteen years ago, summer of 86 or 87, Deacon John took five boys camping up near Boone. During the night, they were attacked by madmen. All five boys were found murdered the next day. Sad but true."

Baffled by his statement, I raise my eyebrow and pry, "What about this makes John a celebrity?"

Smirking, the pastor confides, "The national media was all over the story. Deacon John was on the news for weeks talking about how he was nearly murdered trying to save the boys."

I spring forward in my seat and glare at the pompous demigod. I clear my throat and state, "Let me be clear! Five young boys go camping and are murdered. The adult, who was responsible for their welfare, comes out of the woods alive. The chaperon becomes a celebrity and the boys are forgotten?" I stop talking and shake my head in wonder before declaring, "If I'd been in that same situation, I'd have carried out the dead bodies of the murderers or I wouldn't have come out of the woods at all!"

Pastor Brown looks at me as though I'm a fool. He talks down to me, saying, "I don't set the standards in this country. People watch TV and think anybody they recognize is a celebrity."

I slap the back of the bench in anger and disgust. Choking back saliva, I leer at the pastor and retaliate, "I thought your purpose was to set the records straight? I guess I'm wrong."

Insulted, the pastor rises from the pew, taps his watch and walks away. I get up, catch him and block his path. I ask, "Where can I find John at this hour of the day?"

The pastor sidesteps me and refuses to look up. In a curt voice, he mumbles, "He owns and operates a carpentry shop in Black Mountain. The store is called, Divine Creations."

Pastor Brown abruptly exits the room, goes into his private office and slams the door shut. I leave the building in search of the deacon.

****

Late in the afternoon, I enter the carpentry shop of Divine Creations. As I walk through the store, I observe the assortment of handmade articles. While looking at a wood carved dresser expertly crafted in original design, I sense someone approaching from behind. I turn to acknowledge the figure.

In his late forties, early fifties, and weathered by time, John hasn't aged well. The thick lenses of his horn-rimmed glasses magnify his beady black eyes. His hair is gray and bald on top. His belly puffs out and hangs over the belt of his pants. Even though he is a tall man, his sloppy posture and heavy weight make him appear shorter in height and somewhat stocky in frame.

The churchman walks up to me with a grimace on his face. He extends his hand and announces, "I'm Deacon John Powers. You must be Detective Lee?"

Staring into his eyes, I offer my hand. When we touch, I suffer a jolt to my chest! I stumble backwards and lose my balance! Perspiration beads up on my forehead and palms! I gasp for air as I suffer heart palpitations! John's expression changes to concern as he breaks my fall! He grabs my arm and helps me to a chair! Fighting to catch my breath, I sit down! Both of us are caught off guard by my collapse!

Deacon John frets, "What's wrong with you? Are you having a heart attack? Should I call an ambulance?"

I sit on the wooden seat and wave off his assistance. Struggling to gain control of my body, I gasp, "No, I'm okay. I must be coming down with the flu or something."

John heaves a sigh of relief as he watches the color return to my face. He forgets his hostility and admits, "Pastor Brown called and told me you were at the church asking questions. He warned me to be on the lookout for you."

Having regained most of my strength and composure, I explain, "I've been hired by Betsy Bond to investigate her son's disappearance."

Appearing confused, John confides, "I thought the police determined the boy was a runaway?" He pauses, raises and eyebrow and inquires, "Why, after all these years, has she hired a private detective to come to the same conclusion?"

I rise from the chair, straighten my posture and report, "Betsy doesn't believe Billy ran away. She suspects foul play."

John smiles and patronizes me by concluding, "No mother likes to think her son would run off. But boys run away from home every day of the week."

I don't buy what the deacon is selling. Instead, I continue to interrogate him, inquiring, "I understand you were the last person to see Billy?"

John avoids my eyes. He inhales deeply and replies, "To the best of my recollection, Billy disappeared on a Wednesday night. I took him and some other boys to the movie. When the movie ended, Billy was gone."

Observing his body language, I say, "Please be more specific. What movie? What time did it end? When did you notice Billy missing?"

John continues to avoid eye contact. Appearing to be visualizing the event, he speaks slowly, "The movie was The Matrix with Keanu Reeves. We caught the seven o'clock feature. It ended around nine. Billy was with us when we went in and gone when we came out."

I ask, "What did you do when you realized he was missing?"

The deacon rocks back and forth on his heels. He grimaces as he talks, "Me and the boys looked everywhere for him, inside and outside the theater. Then, we waited in the van for another fifteen or twenty minutes. Since it was getting late and the other boys needed to get home, I drove them back to the church."

Standing erect, I question, "Did you call his mother to see if Billy got home?"

John looks down and examines his fingernails while he answers, "No, I didn't have her phone number."

Frowning, I raise an eyebrow and quip, "That's interesting! You called their house earlier in the day and left a message on the recorder. Did you lose the number after you made the call?"

Angry and defensive at being caught in a lie, John retorts, "No, I didn't lose the damn number!" Taking a moment to think, he reports, "I left it in my office and the building was locked."

I lean over and force John to make eye contact. Challenging his honesty, I probe, "You didn't have a key?"

Embarrassed, the deacon blushes and retaliates, "Of course, I had a key!" He stops talking for a moment and then blurts out, "Look, I wasn't alarmed when Billy left without us! He was from the wrong side of the tracks! Poor folks don't act like normal folks. They have no consideration for other people's feelings."

Scoffing at his explanation, I take a deep breath to control my temper. Then, I question, "Had he ever done anything like that before?"

John glares at me and snarls, "No, but that doesn't mean he wasn't waiting for the right opportunity."

Going in another direction, I ask, "Did you call the police and advise them the boy was missing?"

Getting defensive, John reports, "No, I didn't call the police! Asheville is a small town. Hoodlums don't prowl the streets at night. There was no reason to get the police involved." The big man stops talking and studies my features. Not certain he has justified his actions, he concludes. "You're wasting your time and Betsy's money. Billy got tired of living in poverty and took off. End of story."

Not wanting to totally alienate the witness, I change the subject. Speaking in a civil tone, I ask, "When and why did Billy join your fellowship group?"

Eager to expose the sanctimonious side of his character, John smiles as he reports, "Several times a year, a group of church folk go into Shantytown, a poverty area of the city. We extend a helping hand to children who are conceived in sin and live a filthy existence. I take credit for trying to pull Billy out of that human cesspool."

I'm enraged by John's pious attitude but manage to suppress my anger. In a calm voice, I respond, "You're saying Betsy and her son are white trash?"

Revealing his bigotry, John grins and confides, "I always call a spade a spade."

Suddenly and unexpectedly, I'm overcome with nausea again. The color drains from my face. My knees buckle under me, causing me to fall back in the chair. As I wave the deacon aside, I whisper, "I don't want to keep you from your work. I'll sit here for a few minutes and sneak out when I feel better."

John is oblivious to how offensive I consider his remarks. He's confident his interrogation has been satisfactorily resolved. He doesn't look back as he walks toward the front of the store.

As soon as I feel better, I leave and return to my hotel. After lying down for a few hours, I take a shower and dress in casual attire. I go into the hotel restaurant and espy Maggie sitting at a secluded table. I walk over, sit down and stare at her.

Maggie looks up and meets my gaze. Challenging my detecting skills, she asks, "You're not really surprised to see me, are you?"

I laugh and reply, "Not really. Nothing could surprise me after the day I've had." I take a deep breath and confide, "I met a preacher who takes pride in a coward becoming a celebrity. Then, I had an allergic reaction to this same celebrity which quite literally knocked the wind out of my sails."

Genuinely concerned, Maggie asks, "Are you okay? What happened?"

Dismissing the entire incident, I lean back in my chair and admit, "Yeah, I'm fine. It's no big deal. When the deacon touched me, I got nauseated My body broke a sweat. My knees buckled out from under me. I really thought I was going to throw up."

Maggie is thoughtful for a moment before revealing, "That's odd! Carolyn said Tom had a similar reaction when he came in contact with the deacon."

I shrug my shoulders. Trying to be glib, I suggest, "Maybe, it's his aftershave?" Changing the subject, I ask, "How did you know where to find me?"

Maggie giggles as she replies, "No mystery here. Asheville's a small town." She yawns as she hands me an old, faded newspaper and adds, "Here's a copy of the newspaper you wanted."

I take the paper, lay it on the table and remark, "I'll read it later." Giving in to her charm and tenacity, I ask, "Do you want to come with me tomorrow?"

Maggie yawns again, gets up from the table and replies, "Sounds like a plan. How 'bout I meet you in the lobby at eight?"

I watch Maggie walk out of the restaurant. A waitress approaches the table and takes my order. I eat a light meal before returning to my room. As soon as I get inside, I pick up the telephone and call Bobby. I wait for him to answer. Picking up the receiver on the first ring, he says, "Hello."

Without mincing words, I begin, "I need a background check on John Wesley Powers. I had a negative reaction to him earlier today. I'm getting the same vibes as Maggie. These cases might be connected." I catch my breath and continue, "I need Sam to use his connections and find out how many young boys from North Carolina have been reported missing in the past fifteen years? If he can tap his resources from Atlanta, that's great. If not, I want him to come to Asheville and work from here."

Bobby allows me to finish with my instructions without interruption. Then, he advises, "We'll check it out. Anything else?"

I answer, "No. Get back to me as soon as you have something to report."

I hang up the telephone, sit down on the bed, pick up the newspaper and focus on the headlines. The bold print reads, **FIVE YOUNG BOYS SLAUGHTERED AS CHURCH DEACON FIGHTS FOR HIS LIFE.** I read the article and notice how the journalist managed to play down the murders and tout the deacon. After jotting down the names and addresses of the surviving relatives, I toss the paper aside. Exhausted, I undress, turn off the lights and climb into bed. About midnight, I fall asleep.

I dream, *I'm a young boy. A man with a knife is chasing me through the woods. My legs feel like anchors and weigh me down. I run in slow motion. I see something in the distance. I manage to reach a clearing. All of a sudden, my back hurts. Screaming in pain, I see blood on my hands!*

I wake up with a jolt! I'm in a cold sweat. My back throbs. I look for blood on my hands and am surprised to find them clean and dry. I get up and limp into the bathroom. I take two Aspirins and return to bed. After tossing and turning for what seems like an eternity, I finally fall back to sleep.

Chapter 12

Tracking

Early Wednesday morning, May 14th, Maggie and I go to the local high school. We find the Vice Principal, show him our credentials and advise him of our purpose. The school official agrees to let us interview two boys, Larry and Bart, who were alleged to be with Billy the night he went missing. As we stand in the dean's office waiting, the two teenagers enter the room.

At eighteen, Larry stands five feet eight inches in height and is muscular in form. His brown eyes and dark, shoulder-length hair matches his sullen disposition. As he props his butt on the corner of the table, he gives the distinct impression he comes out of curiosity rather than concern.

Bart is seventeen and mirrors his counterpart's disposition. Standing six feet two inches, he is tall and lanky. His shortly cropped blonde hair compliments his blue eyes and fair complexion. Casual and indifferent, it's obvious he would rather be anywhere but here.

Hoping to quickly dispense with their interview, both boys agree to answer a few questions. I begin, "I'm investigating the disappearance of Billy Bond. I understand you were with him the night he went missing?"

Larry jumps up and retorts, "We may have been at the same movie; but we weren't with Billy!" He hesitates before blurting out, "Neither of us is a fag!"

Surprised by the derogatory innuendo, I look from one boy to the other and ask, "Was Billy gay?"

Slightly embarrassed by his friend's outburst, Bart avoids my eyes and comments, "We don't know for sure. Billy didn't participate in sports. He never talked about guy things. He pretty much kept to himself."

I study the body language of both boys as I direct my next question to Larry, asking, "How did Billy and Deacon John get along?"

Larry thinks about the question before answering, "I'm not sure. Sometimes, I thought he was the deacon's pet. Other times, I felt like they hated each other." He takes a deep breath and confides, "Deacon John is a 'touchy-feely' sort of person. Billy flinched every time he got close to him."

I pick up on Larry's suspicions, walk closer to him and look him in the eyes. Then, I ask, "Did Billy ever say anything about the deacon touching him?"

Larry meets my gaze and blurts out, "No, but something must've happened during the movie 'cause Billy hauled off and socked the deacon! Then, he jumped out of his seat and ran out of the theater!"

Offering support to his friend's statement, Bart leans over and punches Larry's arm. He reports, "Yeah, he punched him just like that.!Then, he ran out of the theater like a bolt of lightning struck him in the ass!"

I'm caught off guard by this new and unexpected information. Eyeing both boys, I ask, "Are you implying the deacon likes boys?" Choosing not to answer, neither boy says a word. After a pregnant pause, I continue my interrogation by stating, "According to the police report, neither of you remembered any of this when they questioned you. Why are your memories razor sharp today?"

Larry and Bart are dumbstruck. They look at each other in disbelief. As soon as the shock factor subsides, Larry exclaims, "The police never ask us nothing!"

Not believing what I'm hearing, I take a step backward. Trying not to show my surprise, I glance at Maggie and frown. Turning back to focus on Larry, I argue, "You're kidding? Right?"

Bart nods. Larry shakes his head, crosses his heart and replies, "I swear to God! No lie!"

Having no more questions, I step aside and

gesture for the boys to go. The counselor orders them to return to class. After the two teenagers are out of hearing range, I thank the school official for his assistance and escort Maggie out of the building.

As we walk to the car, I confess, "When you and Betsy told me the police in Asheville hadn't followed up on the case, I thought you were either uninformed or angry they hadn't found Billy. I apologize for doubting you."

******

After grabbing a quick lunch, Maggie and I head to the poor area of Asheville, known as Shantytown. I park my car in front of a dilapidated old house. We get out and climb the shaky, exterior stairs leading to the front of the building. Maggie shutters as I knock on the door. A frail woman opens the door and invites us inside. The interior is in stark contrast to the exterior, being *white-glove* clean. Pleasantly surprised, Maggie relaxes her posture. She extends her arm to shake the woman's hand.

Looking much older than her forty-eight years, Lilly Campbell is five foot six inches in height and inordinately slender. Her dark hair and eyes accentuate the deep lines on her brow and around her mouth. Starched and ironed, her clothes are as worn as the house's exterior. Although she is well spoken and proud, it's obvious Lilly lives a poor and lonely existence.

Maggie initiates the interview by saying, "Ms.

Campbell, I'm Maggie Harlow. This is Detective Zack Lee. He's been hired by Betsy Bond to investigate the disappearance of her son, Billy. We need to ask you a few questions."

Gesturing for us to sit down, the woman smiles and replies, "Call me Lilly. Everybody else does." Curious, she admits, "I really don't know how I can help? I barely know Betsy. I only saw Billy a couple of times."

I explain, "Betsy doesn't believe Billy ran away. She's afraid something is preventing him from coming home."

Frowning, Lilly agrees, "A mother knows her young'uns. If Betsy says he wouldn't run away, I believe her."

Leaning forward, I state, "The reason I've come to talk with you may be a coincidence or something quite different." I pause, take a deep breath and continue, "Deacon John Powers was with Billy the night he disappeared. I understand he was also the last person to see Rusty alive."

Stiffening her posture, Lilly blurts out, "I wondered if anyone would ever put two and two together!"

Springing forward in her seat, Maggie catches her breath and pries, "Do you think Deacon John killed your son?"

Lilly clutches at her blouse and gasps, "I wouldn't

go that far! But I never understood how he escaped and our boys didn't." She stops talking for a moment and stares into space. When she comes back to reality, Lilly explains, "When I read about his involvement in Billy's disappearance, it certainly aroused my suspicions."

Maggie and I exchange information with Lilly for about an hour. We discuss all the similarities between Billy and Rusty, including their attitudes about attending the church study group. As we rise to leave, I focus on Lilly and inquire, "Have other boys disappeared from this area who haven't been accounted for?"

With a sad expression on her face, Lilly responds, "In the twenty odd years I've lived hereabouts, three or four boys have went missing and not been found."

Curious, Maggie asks, "What happens when the families file missing person reports?"

Lilly shrugs her shoulders and retorts, "What do you think?" Before Maggie has a chance to answer, she elaborates, "The police don't like coming out here. If they do show up, the cops scribble their reports and get out faster than they came in. They pretend to look for the kids; but all of us up here know the truth. If our children are gone, the cops believe they are better off for getting out of here no matter where they went."

Maggie and I don't comment. Lilly explains, "The police are afraid poverty is contagious. They don't want anything to do with us for fear they might become us. Their philosophy is *out of sight, out of mind.*" Tearing up, she elaborates, "There's not a doubt in my mind, if Rusty hadn't been found with those other boys, the local authorities would've chalked him up as another runaway from Shantytown."

I sympathize, "Lilly, you can't blame your personal circumstances for Rusty's murder."

Not wanting pity, Lilly stiffens her posture. Then, she asks, "Do you think the deacon had anything to do with the his death?"

Shaking my head, I answer, "It's too soon in my investigation for me to make such an assumption. But if Deacon John is in any way responsible for the death of Rusty or the disappearance of Billy, I won't stop until I can prove it."

Everyone is quiet for a few moments. Feeling the need to break the silence, I take a deep breath and confide, "The deacon could be a victim of circumstance. But, I'm not going to discount the possibility of his involvement. I'm simply going to follow the clues and let the evidence lead me to the source."

After we say our goodbyes, Maggie and I walk down the stairs, climb into our car and drive away. Lilly watches until we are out of sight. As she walks back inside her house, she recalls our conversation. She is thankful a man and woman with some clout have shown a renewed interest in her loss. For the first time in sixteen years, she thinks there is a chance she might find out who murdered her son.

******

Maggie and I return to the motel and eat dinner. Shortly before eight, we drive to Jason's old neighborhood. I pull into the driveway of a middle-income home. We walk up to the door, knock and wait for an answer. While we stand on the porch, Maggie points across the street and states, "That's where Jason lived before he was murdered."

Our attention is distracted when Jennifer Simmons comes to the door. She opens it and invites us inside. The heavyset woman leads us into the living room where her husband sits in his easy chair.

At forty-nine, Jennifer is an obese woman who takes life's obstacles in stride. Although she laments the death of her son, the stouthearted woman continues to find purpose in life. Rob, fifty-four, is the direct opposite of his wife. He is so emaciated his bones protrude through his skin. His skeletal image reflects his mental state. Existing solely in the shadows of his mind, the grieving father sees no meaning to life.

Introductions are exchanged. Maggie and I are told to refer to the couple by their given names. I begin the interview by explaining, "As you know, Deacon John was the last person to see Jimmy. Recently, I was informed he was also the last person to see Billy Bond. I'm pursuing this common link."

Jennifer stiffens in her chair and challenges, "I

hope you're not implying Deacon John is responsible for the murders. He barely escaped himself. "

I smile to gain her favor and respond, "My job isn't to judge anyone's guilt or innocence. I'm simply gathering information that might help Ms. Bond find Billy."

Embarrassed by her assumption, Jennifer apologizes, "I just want to be clear that you aren't trying to tarnish a good man's reputation." After she's made her point, Jennifer smiles and asks, "What do you need to know?"

I begin my interrogation by stating, "I want to know more about Deacon John as a person. I know he served in Vietnam. Then, moved to Asheville to go into business with a former army buddy, Lone Wolf." I pause and make eye contact with Jennifer before asking, "Do you know this man?"

Jennifer smiles as she reports, "Yes, Lone Wolf is a full-blooded Cherokee. His entire family died in a fire when he was just a boy. He left the reservation and came to Asheville. We went to school together. He's one of the few native American Indians who fought in the Vietnam War." She catches her breath before finishing, "When he came home, he wasn't the same person."

Curious, I inquire, "How so?"

Frowning, Jennifer reports, "Lone Wolf was withdrawn, antisocial. He quit coming to church. When John moved to town, they bought some land in the mountains. They built a couple of cabins and a work shed. The two of 'em worked day and night carving furniture and other specialty items." Jennifer stops and catches her breath before reporting, "A few years after Jimmy and the other boys were murdered, Lone Wolf just disappeared! Nobody has seen or heard from him since!"

Surprised by this revelation, I inquire, "What did John say about his disappearance?"

Jennifer answers, "He said Lone Wolf was involved with some woman from Tennessee. He woke up one morning, went to work and Lone Wolf never showed. John checked his cabin and all his personal effects were gone. He couldn't believe his friend would take off without so much as a fare-thee-well." Jennifer heaves a long, deep sign before finishing, "A few months later, John realized Lone Wolf wasn't coming back. He stayed on the property and opened a shop in Black Mountain."

I glance at Maggie and decide to change the subject. I inquire, "How does Deacon John's fellowship group work? Who chooses the boys? Why is his class the only one offering weekly outings?

Jennifer claps her hands and laughs, "That's easy! Deacon John chooses boys from middle class

146

homes and slum dwellings. He brings them together with hopes of raising the poor child's standards. After Bible class, he takes the boys out for a treat and pays for everything out of his own pocket."

Curious, Maggie asks, "Does Deacon John have a family of his own?"

Jennifer laughs lightly and says, "No, the church is his family. I don't know why he never married and had children. But, I truly believe he is a blessing to this community."

Maggie smiles at Jennifer and inquires, "We can't locate Steve or Charlie's families. Do you know how we might contact them?"

As memories of the past overwhelm her, Jennifer's eyes tear. Crying softly, she gasps, "I never knew Charlie or his family. Steve's family moved to Florida. They didn't leave a forwarding address." She focuses on a picture on the mantel and gasps, "Jimmy and Jason were best friends. Two peas in a pod I always said. After the murders, Carolyn and Tom moved back to Ohio. They asked me to keep them informed of any progress in the case. I never had any news to share."

I look over at Rob who sits staring blankly into space. It's obvious he has no help to offer. Noting my concern, Jennifer explains, "He has been that way since Jimmy died. The murderers should've come to the house and finished him off too. He'd have preferred that to living without his son."

Choking back tears, Maggie shares, "I was still living in Springfield when Tom and Carolyn moved back home. Carolyn managed to move on with her life but Tom suffered from depression."

Curious, Jennifer asks, "Did things get better with time?"

Maggie answers, "No, six months after they moved in with her mother, Carolyn woke up to find Tom dead in bed. Needless to say, Carolyn was heartbroken. But, she lost Tom the moment he was informed of Jason's murder. It just took a little more time to bury him."

Obviously disturbed by Maggie's update, Jennifer shares, "My daughter and I pray Rob will wake up one day and be back to normal. But we know that won't happen until the killers are caught."

Maggie and I leave the Simmons' home, return to the motel and go to our adjoining rooms. As I walk inside my suite, the phone rings. I pick up the receiver and answer, "Hello, this is Zack Lee speaking."

Chapter 13

Discovery

Bobby is on the other end of the line. He begins, "Hi! I hope I'm not disturbing you but I have some interesting news."

I respond, "What?"

Bobby confides, "According to our background check, John Wesley Powers was born in Atlanta on May 23, 1953. This same individual died of pneumonia on June 18, 1955."

Not terribly surprised, I question, "Are you certain we're speaking of the same man?"

Speaking excitedly, Bobby asserts, "I'm proof positive! We verified the birth and death certificates at the Fulton County Court House. John Wesley Powers is buried in a local cemetery alongside his parents."

I confess, "You've got my attention ... go on."

Bobby reveals, "No record of John Wesley Powers surfaces again until sixty-nine. This is when the dead Mr. Powers got a copy of his birth certificate, a social security card and driver's license. He enlisted in the army and served a tour of duty in Vietnam. It was suggested he not reenlist because of questions about his sexuality. He was discharged in 1973."

Wanting to be sure of the facts, I confirm, "Are you absolutely sure this information is valid?"

Bobby replies, "I'm sure. Sam and I went to the cemetery together to view the grave." He stops talking for a few seconds, takes and deep breath and admits, "I have no idea who you're dealing with but the real John Wesley Powers is dead and buried here in Atlanta."

Heaving a deep sigh, I confess, "I don't know why I'm surprised. Nothing about John has rung true; but this information could be most beneficial later on. Thanks for the good work."

I'm quiet for a moment. Interrupting my thoughts, Bobby inquires, "What's on your mind?"

Thinking out loud, I say, "I know we've been hired to investigate the disappearance of Billy; but everything I've uncovered leads back to John." I pause and then continue, "I'm going to go in a different direction. I'm going to where it all began … a campsite in the mountains."

Bobby agrees, "Sounds like a plan. Do you need anything else from this end?"

I answer, "As a matter of fact, I do. Have Sam use his connections to set up an interview with the officer who investigated the murders."

I hang up the telephone. Shortly afterwards, I undress, set the alarm clock, climb into bed and turn out the light. Restless, I toss and turn. Finally, I drift off to sleep. In the wee hours of the night, I'm in the throes of a nightmare.

I'm a young boy lost in the woods. I run in slow motion. It is dark and pouring rain. Flashes of lightning illuminate my surroundings. I hear rumbles of thunder. Something scares me! I start running as fast as I can! Branches and shrubs scratch me! Mud slides beneath my feet! I see something near a tree! I head in that direction to get a closer look! I bend down and crawl on my knees! I'm stabbed in the back! I scream in pain!

I sit straight up in bed. Beads of perspiration wet my forehead. My palms are damp and clammy. My back hurts. I wince in pain. I walk into the bathroom and take two Aspirins. I return to bed, lie on top of the covers and eventually fall back to sleep.

******

Thursday, May 15th, Maggie and I travel to Boone. As we speed up the rural highway, I update her by saying, "John went to the Watauga County Sheriff's Office to report the murders of Jason and the other boys. The sheriff who took the report has agreed to discuss his statement with us."

Maggie and I arrive in the small town at two in the afternoon. I park in front of the police station and we enter the building. A deputy meets us in the lobby and asks us to wait. In a few moments, the sheriff approaches and extends his hand to Maggie and me. After introductions are exchanged, he leads us into his private office.

Sheriff James, now sixty-two, is the classic rural sheriff. He has spent his career keeping local citizens and tourists in line. Occasionally, he puts a few college kids in jail for drinking, driving under the influence and disturbing the peace. His only professional blemish is the unsolved murders of five boys. Nothing would give him greater satisfaction than arresting the killer before he retires.

Anxious to get some specific details, I begin, "I'm investigating a missing person case. A man by the name of John Wesley Powers is involved. This same man is linked to the murders of five boys, which took place in your jurisdiction back in '87. He supposedly came here to file his report. Do you remember the incident?

Sheriff James jumps up from his seat and retrieves an ashtray. He lights a cigarette and exclaims, "How in the world could I ever forget? I remember every detail like it was yesterday!"

I ask, "Will you tell us what happened?"

Sheriff James comes back to his desk and sits down. He exhales smoke as he recalls, "John burst into the station late at night. He was hysterical, crying and screaming about boys being hurt and bleeding. My deputy was on duty alone. He called me and I got here as fast as possible." He catches his breath and continues, "When I got here, the man appeared to be in shock. My deputy thought he had been in a car accident. But when I talked to him, he claimed he and five boys had been attacked in the woods." The sheriff pauses, looks at his cigarette and inhales. As he exhales, he continues, "John asserted he barely escaped with his life but all the boys were dead, stabbed to death. I suspected he was lying about certain details but I couldn't prove it."

I reach into my pocket and retrieve a pack of cigarettes. I offer one to Maggie; but she waves off my gesture. I light one and inhale deeply. Exhaling, I inquire, "Can you recall his physical state?"

Without needing time to think, Sheriff James answers, "John was covered in mud and blood. He had a goose egg on his forehead and several superficial stab wounds." The sheriff stops talking and thinks a moment before adding, "John rarely made eye contact with me. He just stared at his hands."

I probe, "How long did it take you to get to the crime scene?"

Sheriff James extinguishes his cigarette. He gets up and paces as he talks, "We didn't get up there until the next morning 'cause John claimed he couldn't find the campsite in the dark."

As the sheriff continues to pace, I follow his movements with my eyes. I pry, "Didn't you find that a little strange?"

Sheriff James stops pacing, turns and glares at me. His voice raises several octaves as the retorts, "I found it damn strange! However, I had no idea where he'd been. We certainly couldn't find a campsite in these mountains in the dark without a hint as to which way to go. So, we were forced to wait until daylight before we could head up there."

Meeting his eyes, I question, "Did John have any problem finding it in the daylight?"

Without blinking, the sheriff answers, "Nope, no problem at all."

Maggie gets the sheriff's attention by interjecting, "I understand the deacon got a lot of media attention?"

Sheriff James looks at her and snarls, "The news media got wind of the murders and turned the entire area into a circus. John's face was plastered all over the news. You would've thought he was some kind of celebrity when he was a coward at best and murderer at worst."

Getting back on track, I inquire, "What were the weather conditions in respect to gathering evidence?"

Frowning, Sheriff James responds, "The weather couldn't have been worse. A heavy downpour saturated the entire area. It thundered and lightened all night. The coroner estimated the times of death between eight and midnight." Feeling the need to be more specific, the police officer elaborates, "The rain started about nine and didn't let up until morning. If there had been any fingerprints, footprints or tire marks, they were washed away before we arrived on the scene."

I extinguish my cigarette while Maggie asks, "Who did John say killed the boys?"

Sheriff James starts pacing again. Shrugging his shoulders, he replies, "He didn't. He claimed he was assaulted first. Supposedly, he didn't see his assailant and had no clue how many there were?"

I raise an eyebrow and suggest, "It appears you are suspicious of John. Would that be a correct assumption on my part?"

Sheriff James glares at me. Totally frustrated, he exclaims, "Damn straight! I didn't believe one word that came out of his mouth then and I still don't! How can a man be struck from the front and not see who hit him?" As Maggie and I sit listening to his words, the sheriff continues to vent. He pounds his fist on the desk and declares, "The big problem is motive! We are dealing with a pillar of the church community, a deacon no less. He has an impeccable reputation and uses his own money to finance outings for young boys. It would take more evidence than I've been able to gather to even cast aspersions on his character, much less convict him of murder."

Everyone in the room is thoughtful and quiet for a few moments. I break the silence by stating, "I'd like to see the crime scene. Will you take Maggie and me to the campsite?" As the sheriff mulls over my question, I feel the need to put all my cards on the table. I state my case by confiding, "I don't have a clue what happened to Billy but I believe John committed these five murders and possibly others we don't even know about? And, I've promised two mothers I won't rest until I have answers to a whole lot of questions."

Sheriff James grabs my hand, shakes it and exclaims, "At last, a man after my own heart! I'll take you up there first thing in the morning." Smiling mischievously, he adds, "There's a catch though! If you gather enough evidence to get a warrant, I want to be the one to arrest John. So, it will be your responsibility to lure him back to Boone. Do we have a deal?"

In agreement, we shake hands and seal the deal. Without further discussion, Maggie and I leave his office in search of a motel. I rent adjoining rooms. After carrying in our luggage, we leave to find a nearby restaurant. After dinner, Maggie comes back to my room with me. We talk about everything from the case to our personal lives. When the hour grows late, Maggie yawns and makes excuses for her fatigue. She gets up, leaves the door ajar and disappears into her own room.

I undress, turn on the television and watch it for a while. When I get tired, I turn it off and settle in bed. As soon as I fall asleep, the recurring nightmare creeps into my sleep state. While my astral body wrestles in the spirit world, my physical body thrashes around in bed.

I'm an adolescent boy. I look down and notice the pockets of my yellow nylon jacket have zippers. I see a tear in my jeans. My tennis shoes are spattered with mud. I hold a small flashlight in my right hand and a compass in my left. I'm being chased by a man with a knife and run in slow motion. Lightning illuminates my surroundings. I spy a body, lying at the base of a large tree. I run over and kneel down. I touch it and check for signs of life. I cry out as a knife pierces my back. I suffer a second blow and everything goes dark . Strangely, I don't die. I float behind and above my assailant. I follow the dark figure through the forest. I watch him reach a car and bury something under a tree. The Pine tree is vividly clear. The features of the man are vague.

Maggie is awakened by my screams. She hears my shrill, piercing cries and barges into my room! Trembling, she turns on the light. Seeing me thrashing around in bed, she rushes over to my bedside. My face is drained of color and perspiration saturates my forehead. Maggie shakes me until I open my eyes. Awakening from my night terror, I grab her arm! Holding it tightly, I sit up and try to focus my eyes!. As soon as I'm alert and cognizant, I relax my grip.

Maggie gasps, "What in the world is going on? You nearly scared me to death! I thought someone was trying to kill you!"

After scanning the room, I realize I was only dreaming. My heart rate slows. I take a moment to catch my breath before I confess, "I was having that nightmare again. I must've been talking in my sleep."

Still reeling from the frightening experience, Maggie collapses on the bed. She corrects me, stating, "You weren't talking. You were screaming."

I get out of bed and put on my trousers. I dig in my suitcase and remove a pack of cigarettes. I put one to my lips and light it. I inhale deeply and allow the smoke to fill my lungs. As I exhale, I blow smoke rings in the air. When my nerves settle, I walk over to the edge of the bed and sit down beside Maggie. Apologetic, I say, "I'm sorry I scared you. I've been having a recurring dream. It gets more vivid and frightening each time I dream it."

Maggie asks, "When did the dream start? Why is it so frightening?"

Taking her into my confidence, I state, "The nightmare started the night I met Deacon John. It …" Suddenly, a light goes off in my head. I stop talking. I'm thoughtful for a few moments. Then, I correct myself by admitting, "That's not true. They actually started after I was involved in a car accident."

Speaking softly, Maggie pries, "Do you want to

talk about it?"

I look intently at Maggie and sigh. Appreciative of her concern, I explain, "While I was in the hospital recuperating, I was plagued with nightmares. I dreamt I was killed in an auto accident. Then, I was murdered by a man with a knife. The cycle went back and forth for months. Finally, the dreams stopped."

Watching me extinguish my cigarette and light another one, Maggie inquires, "Did you experience any other anomalies?"

Ignoring her question, I conclude, "To be quite blunt, I was acting so crazy my aunt almost had me committed to a mental institution." Opening her eyes wide, Maggie doesn't comment. I go on, "I was like two people. I'd be really nice one day and an asshole the next. My aunt got so concerned she gave me two options, take a leave of absence from work or get well wearing a straight jacket. I always hated clothes that bind, so I opted for door number one."

Maggie asks, "If you were that bad off, why did she give you a choice?"

I search Maggie's eyes and look deep into her soul. Trusting my instincts, I answer, "After I was back to normal, my aunt explained that I told her something the first time I woke up which really impressed her. It made such an impact she was willing to negotiate my method of treatment."

Curious, Maggie pries, "What did you tell her??"

I wave my finger under her pretty nose and answer, "I'm willing to share; but I'm not an open book. That's between my aunt and me."

Intrigued by my story, Maggie pries, "Besides the nightmares and split personality, did you do anything else out of the ordinary?"

I press the lit end of my cigarette against the base of the ashtray as I confess, "There are two incidents that jump out at me." Slightly embarrassed, I avoid Maggie's eyes as I recall, "I put a woman in jail for murdering her daughter. Her husband hated my guts. I dropped by his house one day to tell him I was sorry."

I wait for Maggie's reaction. She doesn't react. Seeing no reason to stop now, I'm compelled to expel all of my demons. I blurt out, "I was intimately involved with a married woman. I ended the relationship by calling her a whore. Six months later, I handed her a check for five thousand dollars and told her to get a life." Wanting to end the discussion, I exclaim, "To sum it up, I didn't know whether to shit or get off the pot!"

Maggie smiles at me. She starts giggling. Her eyes twinkle. Laughing out loud, she jokes, "Well, it looks like you've got your shit together now!"

I watch Maggie laugh. Finding her laughter

contagious, I burst out laughing myself. Caught up in the humor of the moment, I pick up a pillow and swat her. She gets the other pillow and hits me back. We compete in an old-fashioned pillow fight. Exhausted, we fall back on the bed. Maggie positions herself on her elbow and pecks me on the cheek. I respond by pulling her close and giving her a kiss. The kiss becomes sensual. Passion erupts. Leaning over to extinguish the bedside light, I admit, "I promised myself I wouldn't let this happen."

Out of the darkness, Maggie whispers, "Sometimes promises are made to be broken."

Chapter 14

Crime Scene

The day is Friday, May 16th. Anxious to visit the crime scene, Maggie and I rise at dawn. We hurriedly dress, grab a bite in the motel restaurant and head for our meeting with the sheriff. On the way, I spy a hardware store as it opens for business. I pull in the parking lot, park the car and look over at Maggie. Slightly embarrassed, I grin as I say, "I know you're gonna think I'm a nutcase but I need to express my thoughts. The recurring nightmare I've been having are gnawing at my gut. And, to be honest, I feel like the ghost of one of those murdered boys is trying to tell me something or possibly show me something." Relieved that Maggie isn't rolling her eyes or frowning, I have the courage to go on, "Last night, every detail of my dream was so vivid it seemed real. Today, we're heading for the woods. I think this might be where my nightmare takes place. Am I crazy for thinking I might find myself in the exact spot where the terrifying experience occurs?"

Maggie notes the strain in my voice and

responds, "I don't believe in coincidence. I think everything happens for a purpose. If you really believe your dream relates to this case, do whatever it takes to prove it."

Thankful for her logic, I go inside the building. In a few minutes, I return carrying a bag of cold drinks and a shovel. I place the tool in the trunk and put the bag in the backseat. After following his directions, we meet up with Sheriff James. Right away, he suggests we follow him in our vehicle. He explains, "We're doing this on the Q.T. If I'm called to duty or have an accident, I don't want to have to explain my actions." As I turn my car around, the sheriff hollers, "The drive will take about forty-five minutes."

Sheriff James climbs in his patrol car and heads west. I follow closely behind. In less than an hour, we pull off the rural highway and turn onto a gravel road. As our cars ascend the mountainous terrain, Maggie gets nervous. The reality of seeing the place where Jason was murdered fills her with dread. As yesterday's sorrow surfaces anew, tears flow from her eyes. Unable to ignore her miserable state, I hand Maggie a handkerchief and sympathize, "You don't have to do this. If you want to wait in the car, I'll understand."

In a trembling voice, Maggie insists, "I've got to face the past. It's the only way I'll ever have a future."

Sheriff James stops his car when he reaches an old, metal gate. He gets out of his vehicle, unlatches the wire fastening and swings the rickety barrier open. He climbs back into his car and proceeds up the narrow winding dirt road. I continue to follow. Within minutes, both of us park under several tall trees. The three of us get out and survey the isolated area. Sheriff James points as he talks, "Over there by that big Pine tree is where John parked his van before he and the boys headed off into the woods." Focusing on our faces, he announces, "It's about two miles to the campsite. Some of the trail is pretty rough. Are y'all ready and able to walk that far?"

Making eye contact with the sheriff, Maggie responds, "I'm as ready as I'll ever be."

I signal for a time out. I return to my car and retrieve the bag of drinks. I open it and hand one to Maggie and toss another to the sheriff. I get my own water bottle before throwing the bag back inside my car. Then, I turn and say, "Lead the way."

We begin our hike through the woods. Several times, we pause to drink and catch our breath. After nearly an hour of walking over rough terrain, we reach a clearing shadowed by a huge Oak tree. Our guide stops and points as he talks, "This is where we found the first two boys. It appears the one propped against the tree died first. He had defensive wounds, indicating he fought his assailant. The second boy was stabbed in the back. He had no defensive wounds.."

As I survey the area, I ask, "Which two boys?"

Sheriff James pulls a manila envelope out of his jacket. He removes several wrinkled photos. He reads the notes on the back of the pictures. Handing them to me, he answers, "The boy leaning against the tree is Jimmy Simmons. The other boy is Jason Frazier."

I try to shield the photographs; but Maggie catches a glimpse of the morbid pictures. She gasps in horror. Tears stream down her cheeks. Turning away, Maggie motions for the sheriff and me to leave her alone. After her hysteria passes, she wipes her eyes and apologizes, "I'm sorry for my outburst." Then, she straightens her posture and announces, "I'm ready to go on."

Sheriff James takes the lead position and guides us through the woods. The trail is difficult to traverse as it hasn't been used in years. After more than thirty minutes of fighting nature's obstacles, we reach the campsite. Each one of us takes a moment to survey the site. The underbrush has nearly covered the area. The cabin looks like it's ready to cave in. The water in the stream laps against the shoreline as the wind whistles through the trees. The setting is eerily serene.

Breaking the silence, Sheriff James begins walking and pointing as he speaks. He says, "This used to be a fairly popular campsite until the murders. Then, campers started claiming they saw ghosts here at night. Word got out that the place was haunted. Now, nobody comes here."

Using photographs to remind him of the details, Sheriff James directs our attention to specific areas. Speaking in spurts, he says, "Steve was found near the campfire. Apparently, he confronted the killer and fought back. He had numerous defensive wounds. Charlie was over yonder. He must've been running when he was stabbed in the back. Rusty was next to that boulder. Although he died of a stab wound like the others, it appears he was the primary target." Resting his hands on his hips, Sheriff James stands in place. Looking at me, he states, "Rusty was beaten pretty badly before he was stabbed. And, according to the autopsy report, he was sexually molested. There was bleeding indicating the assault was recent but scar tissue suggest it was not the first time he had been sexually abused."

I listen to the new details of the case. I'm sickened by the pictures, the murder scene and confirmation of Rusty's sexual abuse. Trying to control my emotions, I make a mental note I'm here to gather information not react by making rash judgments. Because of her personal relationship with Jason, Maggie's emotional state is numb. She doesn't comment about the details. She is wearing her business face and mentally filing the facts away for future reference. The sheriff kicks dirt with his boot to vent his frustration. He is still disappointed that the killer got away. Revisiting the murder scene has rekindled his desire to solve the case.

Trying to visualize the events as they might have happened, I speculate, "Five boys sit around a campfire. The only adult is supposedly down by the stream. Let's buy his story and say he was attacked while he was alone. It would've been impossible for one man to stab John, run back to camp, molest and beat Rusty, fight off Steve and catch Charlie, killing each of them as they go?" Maggie and the sheriff don't comment. I offer another scenario, postulating, "Even if this scenarios was possible, how did the killer know two boys got away? More to the point, how would he be able to track two boys in a vast forest in a blinding rain?"

Nodding his head in agreement, Sheriff James declares, "That's the sixty-four thousand dollar question?" He takes a deep breath before surmising, "We can speculate until the end of time but we won't be one step closer to the truth. And, speculation doesn't put a murderer behind bars. The only way we will ever know the truth is if John confesses or an eyewitness falls into our laps. I'm a betting man, but I wouldn't take those odds."

After spending a few more minutes checking out the campsite, the three of us head back to our cars. As we approach the clearing where Jason and Jimmy were found, I notice some rubble. Pointing, I ask, "What's that pile of wood over there?"

Sheriff James glances in that direction and answers, "When I came here to investigate the murders, it was an outhouse. I guess time has caused it to collapse." He pauses for a moment and then recalls, "A few years back, I brought one of those psychics up here that helped police solve other murders. She offered little to nothing to help solve this case."

Looking at the sheriff, Maggie asks, "She didn't get any vibes at all?"

Grimacing, Sheriff James answers, "She claimed to see a ghost ... a young boy ... climb out of the outhouse and run to the tree where Jimmy and Jason were found. She described him as wearing a yellow jacket, torn jeans and dirty tennis shoes." He hesitates a moment before adding, "The ghost gave her the distinct impression he was looking for something."

As I hear the words... yellow ... jacket ... my heart skips a beat. Unable to speak, I glance at Maggie. Reading my mind, she asks, "Were any of the murdered boys wearing a yellow jacket?"

The sheriff pulls the pictures out of his pocket and studies his notes. Reading aloud, he says, "Second boy, Jason Frazier, wearing yellow jacket, torn jeans and white tennis shoes." As the reality of the psychic's vision hits home with the sheriff, he slaps himself on the forehead and gasps, "I should've caught that earlier! I guess it's too late now!"

Maggie and I stare at each other but don't say a word. Not wanting to share my nightmare with the sheriff, I keep my mouth shut. Maggie and I follow our guide out of the woods. About one-thirty, we make it back to our starting place. As he heads for his car, Sheriff James notices Maggie and I are standing still. Puzzled, he inquires, "Aren't you two ready to go?"

I respond, "Maggie wants to say a final farewell to Jason." As the sheriff starts to object, I add, "Don't worry, we'll leave in a few minutes."

Sheriff James shrugs his shoulders, walks to his car and climbs inside. He starts the engine, backs up, turns around and waves as he drives away. When he is out of sight, I open the trunk of my car and grab the shovel. I walk over to the enormous Pine tree and start digging. As I dig holes in the dirt, Maggie watches.

After digging and sweating profusely for nearly an hour, my shovel gets caught in debris. I drop to my knees and start digging with my hands. I retrieve a rusty knife. Remnants of rotten, green cloth cling to the blade. At the same moment, Maggie notices a glint of metal. She bends over and unearths a pair of rusty eyeglasses. She picks them up and jumps for joy. I watch Maggie dancing in circles, giggling with delight. In a somber voice, I warn, "Don't get too excited. This evidence isn't going to send John to the gas chamber."

Disappointed by my remark, Maggie argues, "What do you mean?"

I look up from my knees and wipe the dirt off my hands. I scoop up the evidence and rise to my feet. In a solemn voice, I explain, "There couldn't possibly be any fingerprints on this knife after being buried all these years. Even if there were, I'm sure John would admit it was his."

Maggie argues, "It certainly raises questions as to

why it was buried?"

Rolling my eyes, I answer, "Yeah, and it raises even more questions as to how I found it. It's actually more incriminating against me than John." As Maggie looks at me in wonder, I take a deep breath and explain, "I was sixteen when the boys were murdered. I could literally become the prime suspect. And, no judge in the country would buy the story I dreamt about it being buried in this exact spot."

Maggie looks at me in disbelief. I pick up the shovel and start filling in the holes. As she watches me work, Maggie retorts, "What do you suggest?"

I don't answer her question. I continue to shovel dirt as Maggie concentrates on our dilemma. Out of the blue, she has a brainstorm. Eager to share, she blurts out, "Were you paying attention when the sheriff was talking about that psychic? How she claimed to see a ghost run out of the shed and over to the tree, looking for something?"

I stop filling holes and answer, "Yeah, and she described the clothes Jason was wearing to a tee."

As I lean on my shovel, Maggie talks more to herself than me. She theorizes, "The ghost had to be Jason. So, what was he looking for?" I see the wheels turning in Maggie's head. Suddenly, she recalls, "I gave Jason a necklace and locket before he moved to Asheville. Carolyn told me he never took it off. When his body was recovered, those items were missing.

They must've been lost or stolen. Don't you see? This is what the ghost is searching for!"

Frowning, I ask, "Where are you going with all this mumbo-jumbo?"

Maggie remains quiet as she stares at the rusty knife. She is lost in thought. Suddenly, she lets out a cry and gasps, "Let's tell the sheriff you lost your Rolex. We backtracked through the woods. When we reached the woodpile, you saw your watch on the ground. You bent down to pick it up and spotted a knife under the wood. After you examined it, we decided to look for more evidence. A few minutes later I found the eyeglasses." I stand and listen while Maggie theorizes, "This should whet the sheriff's appetite. He will be compelled to send a search team up there to look for anything we might have missed."

Staring at Maggie, I ask, "What do you hope to find?"

Maggie meets my gaze and responds, "I don't know! Jason's necklace and locket, anything that might point the finger at John." Catching her breath, she continues, "I don't have the answer but my feminine intuition is telling me something is up there and we can find it if we look."

Considering all the strange things that have happened to me in the past five years, I actually consider Maggie's plan. Staring at her, I warn, "You realize we'll be tampering with evidence?"

Frustrated, the young woman rolls her eyes in disbelief. Undaunted by my warning, Maggie challenges, "Do you honestly believe we'd be the first two people in history to alter a few details to catch a murderer?" Determined to make her case, she declares, "Besides, that psychic saw the ghost for a reason! The reason could be as simple as giving us a place to look!"

Maggie stops talking and stares at me. In a soft voice, she pleads, "I gave you the benefit of the doubt when you told me about your dream. I didn't say you were crazy when you bought that shovel." As her voice gets louder, she persists, "I'm willing to bend a few rules if it puts a murderer in jail! Are you?"

I take a few moments to consider all the possibilities. Although my head is saying no, my gut is saying yes. I decide there is nothing to lose but a few more hours in the woods. So, I surrender to Maggie's charm and say, "Give me a few minutes to fill in these holes and cover them with leaves. Then, we will hike back up to the woodpile and move some wood around."

Chapter 15

Evidence

It is nearly noon on Saturday, May 17th. Watching two officers sift through warped, decayed boards and toss them aside, Maggie and I stand next to Sheriff James. He remarks, "I remember John wasn't wearing a coat when he came in the station. I thought that was odd 'cause the weather was brisk and rainy. When I asked him about being cold, he claimed he lost his jacket and knife in the woods." The sheriff stops talking, lights a cigarette and continues, "He wasn't wearing eyeglasses but nothing was mentioned about 'em.."

I comment, "He gave you this information voluntarily. A good lawyer could make the case the items were hidden by the assailants."

Frowning, Sheriff James glances at me and asks, "What about motive?"

I quickly respond, "It sure wasn't about money. It had to be personal."

The three of us watch the officers dismantle the woodpile. As I gaze at the workers, I think about Betsy and Lilly. Sharing information, I report, "According to Ms. Bond, when Billy started going to church he was happy to go. Later and with no explanation, he didn't want to go back. Two boys in the class claimed John was always trying to touch him. But, Billy didn't like it. The night he went missing, Billy came to blows with John. These same boys witnessed their altercation."

Sheriff James probes, "What about Rusty?"

I answer, "Rusty's mother repeated the same behavior almost verbatim. At first, he enjoyed the church activities and wanted to be a part of the group. Later, his mother had to force him to go." I catch my breath and continue, "Rusty and his mother had always been close. Suddenly and for no apparent reason, he quit confiding in her and demanded his privacy. Billy did the same thing shortly before he went missing."

Maggie surmises, "You're suggesting both boys were being sexually molested by the deacon?"

Sheriff James glances at Maggie and states, "According to the autopsy report, Rusty was being sexually abused. This is a scientific fact." He drops his cigarette and stomps on it with his boot as he goes on, "This could be the motive for killing Rusty and possibly Billy. But, it doesn't explain the murders of the other boys. According to their autopsies, none of them were being molested. "

I speculate, "I understand this discrepancy but let's assume John is a pedophile. It goes without saying he wouldn't approach every boy in his class. He'd come on to the boys with the lease amount of self worth." I pause before continuing, "Poor boys are usually raised by single mothers who would be impressed that their sons were getting special attention from an adult male, a religious figure no less. They would encourage their sons to look up to him and trust him like a father."

Nodding his head, Sheriff James agrees with my hypothesis and adds, "By choosing boys from poverty areas, nobody questions John's motives. They assume he's offering his time and attention for the sake of religion."

Maggie looks sick and disgusted as she listens to the conversation. She turns her attention away from us and watches the deputies lift the last board off the pile. Then, the men pick up shovels and form dirt heaps. This process becomes time consuming. Nothing surfaces. Tiring, one officer moves to take a break. He stumbles over the cement blocks. One square falls and lands on its side. Cussing his clumsiness, the man bends down to rub his ankle. He notices a rusty canteen protruding out of the block. He reaches down, picks it up and starts to toss it into the woods. As he lifts it in the air, he hears a rattling sound. Curious, he twist open the cap and peers inside. He sees note paper. He starts to pull it out.

The sheriff sees him and shouts, "Dave, don't do that! Put the canteen back where you found it! Steve get the camera and take pictures. Then, I'll remove whatever is inside!"

Everyone is stunned by the discovery. All of us gather around the area as Steve snaps pictures. Sheriff James gently pulls the paper out of the canteen. Then, he turns the container upside down. A small necklace and locket fall into his hand. Maggie points and gasps, "Oh, my God! That looks like the necklace and locket I gave Jason!"

After all the excitement subsides, the sheriff takes command. He drops the jewelry back into the canteen and seals it. Then, he gently folds the note paper and stuffs it in his pocket. His men gather their tools and the group of us hikes back to our starting point. Anxious to scrutinize the evidence, every member of the search team hurries to their cars. Plans are made to meet back at the police station later in the day. Afterwards, everyone heads down the mountain.

******

Maggie and I arrive at the station about three. We go straight to the sheriff's office. Sheriff James, a deputy and stenographer are waiting for us. As soon as we walk in the room, everyone takes a seat. Sheriff James begins, "I've asked Ms. Burch to sit in on this meeting. She is going to witness the procedure and take notes." As he talks, the sheriff unscrews the cap of the canteen. He turns it upside down and allows the jewelry to fall out onto his desk. He picks up the jewelry and hands it to Maggie, inquiring, "Can you identify these items?"

Maggie carefully examines the jewelry and hands it back to the sheriff. Tearing up, Maggie whispers "Yes, this is the necklace and locket I gave Jason Frazier before he moved to Asheville." She takes a deep breath and adds, "If you open the case, you'll see our pictures."

Following her suggestion, Sheriff James takes the locket and gently pries it open. Then, he hands it back to Maggie and inquires, "Can you identify the people in the photos?"

Pointing at the images, Maggie responds, "Yes, I'm the one on the right. Jason is on the left."

Sheriff James takes the jewelry out of Maggie's hand and lays it on his desk. He carefully unfolds the handwritten note. He uses paperweights to spread it out. He motions for his deputy to take pictures of each sheet. Obviously surprised by its good condition, he comments, "I'm amazed at what good condition this letter is in after being in a canteen for nearly sixteen years." Looking at Maggie, the sheriff inquires, "Can you identify the handwriting?"

Maggie gets up, leans over the desk and studies the penmanship. After carefully examining the note, she reports, 'Yes, it looks like Jason's handwriting."

Sheriff James acknowledges Maggie's response and indicates to the stenographer to record her answer. Glancing over at the deputy, he orders, "Dave, turn on the tape recorder." He puts on his glasses and begins reading, "My name is Jason Frazier. I came on a camping trip with Deacon John, Steve, Charlie, Jimmy and Rusty. We were having a great time until Rusty got REAL upset ..."

****

Rusty stands in front of the fire. Holding his hands behind his back, he rocks back and forth on his heels, glaring at the deacon. All of us boys look up and acknowledge him but our chaperone pays him no attention. Extremely agitated, Rusty expels his anger by screaming, " You perverted bastard! You sit here and preach religion, when you are the devil himself!"

Deacon John ignores Rusty's insult. The youngster stomps his foot in anger! Rage engulfs him and takes control of his actions! He screams and runs at the deacon! As he brandishes the hunting knife menacingly, the rest of us are startled as the firelight catches the glitter of the blade! We sit paralyzed on the ground and don't make a sound! The deacon has his back to Rusty and doesn't see the weapon! He makes no attempt to get out of the way! Running, Rusty screams, "You've put your filthy hands on me for the last time!"

The boy stabs the deacon in the shoulder! The big man screams in shock and pain! He jumps up and grabs for the knife! Rusty manages to slash his hand before being subdued! Deacon John jerks the knife out of his clutches! The youngster

180

becomes hysterical, screaming and sobbing as he gasps, "I hate you! I hate you! I'm going to tell every member of the church what you've been doing to me!"

As blood dampens his shirt, Deacon John holds Rusty firmly in his grasp! Wincing in pain, he turns to look at us and shakes his head! We stand spellbound, caught in the surreal moment! None of us moves or speaks, hoping if we don't acknowledge the assault it will vanish like a ghost in the night! The deacon exclaims, "I have no idea what Rusty is talking about! He has lost his ever loving mind!" He continues to hold tight to the boy, speaking in gasps, "I've given this boy the same spiritual guidance as the rest of you! I've tried to teach him right from wrong but what can you expect from a child who crawled out of Shantytown?"

Rusty becomes rabid with rage! He looks from Jimmy to Steve as he fights for the truth, screaming, "Bull shit! Has he screwed you, Jimmy? What about you, Steve? Has he forced you to suck his cock?" Jimmy and Steve shake their heads, while Charlie and me remain transfixed! Rusty continues to fight for the truth, yelling, "Yeah, that's what I thought! The good deacon prefers to get down and dirty with the trash!".

Deacon John spins around and knocks Rusty to the ground! He is no longer concerned about witnesses! As he kicks the boy over and over again, the deacon shouts and hisses, "You little candy ass! I've been nothing but kind to you! I pulled you out of the gutter! I gave you a taste of the good life! This is how you repay me? Trying to shame me! Making me out to be some kind of monster!" The big man stops kicking Rusty, backs away and takes a deep breath! Fighting to gain control of the situation, *he spits out orders, "Pull yourself together and admit to these boys you are lying!"*

I'm speechless! I can't believe what I'm hearing and seeing! It is like watching a scary movie in slow motion! I just want the whole thing to go away and forget it happened!

Rusty is consumed with hatred for his abuser! He feels defiled! He has tried to wash away the awful memories, scrubbing his body so hard it bleeds; washing his clothes in bleach; ironing them at the highest setting! But, nothing works! The stench of Deacon John has permeated his very existence! Nothing makes the pain go away! Nothing blurs the reality of being molested over and over again by the monster that is making a mockery of religion!

Rusty's temper is as explosive as a stick of dynamite! All the anger he has bottled up erupts into a frenzy of emotions! The bruised and beaten boy climbs to his feet, scales a large boulder and lunges at the deacon! Oblivious to the knife in his hand, Deacon John takes a defensive stance! Rusty lands on the blade! The force of his weight propels the deacon backward! He falls to the ground, pinned under the boy! Rusty is motionless!

Claustrophobia overcomes fear! Struggling to breathe, Deacon John pushes the boy aside, rolling his body over and crawling out from under it! He becomes spasmodic and crawls backward on his haunches until his retreat is blocked by a tree! The horrible truth is suddenly exposed! Deacon John's hunting knife is buried in the boy's chest! Dumbfounded, everyone watches in silence as Rusty exhales his final breath!

I can't take my eyes off the body! My heart stops and blood drains from my face! I gasp for air as it starts beating again, pounding in my ears! I look from Jimmy to Steve to Charlie, hoping I've imagine what I've seen! Each face confirms the hard, cold facts! All of us are witness to murder! Steve is the first person to regain his wits. He sprints over to Rusty, kneels down and begins CPR. Although he gets no response, the teenager continues in his efforts. Deacon John pulls him off the lifeless body. He leans down and feels for a pulse. He jerks the knife out of Rusty's body and stands upright. The weapon dangles by his side as the deacon reports, "You're wasting your energy. He's dead."

Dazed and confused, I get up off the ground. Jimmy and Charlie stand up beside me. None of us offer to help him. Instead, we stand paralyzed, looking into the face of a man who has become a very real threat. Deacon John sobs for a few moments. He wipes his eyes with the sleeve of his jacket. He winces and moans, "There's no reason to be afraid of me. Rusty fell on the knife. I didn't stab him on purpose. I didn't mean to kill him."

Steve is aware our survival hangs in the balance. He is frightened but fights his own fear in an effort to protect the rest of the boys. Signaling us with his eyes, Steve agrees with the deranged man. Speaking softly, he says, "We know that. It was a horrible accident."

Deacon John scrutinizes us while he listens to Steve. He sees fear and anger in our eyes. Slowly, it dawns on him that he might have to answer for his crime. He could be ostracized from the church. Worse still, he could actually go to jail. Everything depends on what we say. If our stories differ from his, the deacon will be the one to pay … not us. As a ploy for sympathy, the wounded man touches his shoulder and shows us the blood on his hand. *Getting no reaction, he begins to panic. He protests, "As God is my witness, I would never do the awful things Rusty said. Y'all know he was lying, right?" Looking from one boy to the next, he frets, "Rusty was a sick twisted boy. I should never have pulled him out of the gutter. I should have left him in that cesspool he called home."*

The silence is deafening. Determined to win some sympathy, the deacon declares, "I'm a good man! I'm the victim here ... not Rusty!"

Trying to gain his confidence, Steve lies, "We know that. Don't worry about us."

Glancing at Steve, Deacon John admits, "I had to defend myself." Turning to look at us, he continues, "Y'all saw ..." Without finishing his sentence, he stops talking. He takes a step toward us. We back up. He takes another step forward and we back up again. The deacon realizes he is being duped. He knows his words are falling on deaf ears.

Sensing his anguish and desperation, Steve offers, "Why don't you give me the knife and let me help you?"

Steve's condescending manner is beginning to gall the man. Suspicious of his motives, Deacon John challenges, "Who do you think you are? I'm the adult here ... not you!" Becoming more paranoid, he adds, "Don't treat me like a child or a 'Looney tune.' I'm in control here ... not you!"

Charlie whimpers. Steve glances at him and motions for him to hush. As soon as Steve takes his eyes off the deacon, the big man raises the knife and stabs him in the chest. As he struggles to keep his balance, Steve screams, "RUN! RUN FOR YOUR LIVES!"

Steve falls to his knees! He holds his arms over his head in a defensive position! Deacon John stabs him several more times! He collapses on the ground! The deacon whirls around and sees Charlie running toward the trail! He chases him down, catches up and stabs him in the back! Jimmy and me race for the creek! When we get close to the water, we crawl under some bushes! A few moments later, we see the deacon approaching with his flashlight! He stops near our hiding place and listens intently! We hold our breath! Splashing sounds come from the creek! The big man heads in that direction! We watch from our vantage point as the deacon stands on a large rock and shouts, "Jimmy! Jason! Don't be afraid! I won't hurt you!"

Suddenly and unexpected, the deacon slips off the rock! He falls and hits his head! Both of us hear the thud! The flashlight goes dark and silence prevails! Jimmy and me remain in place for several minutes! When the deacon doesn't move, we crawl out from under the bushes and run back to camp! From the glow of the dwindling fire, we can see our three friends lying in pools of blood. I tiptoe over to Steve, fall to my knees and feel for a pulse. Getting no heartbeat, I shake my head at Jimmy and rise to my feet. Then, I walk slowly over to Charlie and bend down. Again, I feel for a pulse and get no response. Jimmy begins to cry. I speak barely above a whisper, ordering, "This is not the time or place to cry! We don't know if the deacon is dead or alive! We need to get away from here as fast as possible!"

I sprint over to the spot where I was lying before all Hell broke loose. I grab my jacket and put it on. Then, I retrieve my miniature flashlight and compass out of the pocket. It begins to rain. As soon as I determine which way to go, I shout, "Come on Jimmy, let's get out of here!"

Jimmy and me make our way through the woods. The rain continues to pour, drenching the area. We slip and slide as we make our way through the woods. At one point, Jimmy falls in a rabbit hole and twists his ankle. He can still walk but the injury slows us down. When we stop for a moment to catch our breath, the two of us sit down on a fallen tree. Jimmy takes the opportunity to express his thoughts, suggesting, "If the deacon comes after us, we need to split up. He might get one of us but the other one can still get away."

I retaliate, "I can't leave you! You're my best friend!"

Red-faced, tired and in pain, Jimmy argues, "One of us needs to get out of here alive so the deacon won't get away with murder! Promise me you'll run for your life if we hear him coming!"

Seeing the determination in his eyes, I nod my head and agree to the plan. After a short rest, we continue making our way through the woods. Suddenly and unexpected, we hear a rustle in the woods behind us! Jimmy cries out, "Run, Jason! Run!"

I run until I'm out of breath. A flash of lightning exposes the area. Much to my shock and relief, I see the lean-to we passed earlier in the day. I run to the building and climb inside. The rain pours down. Thunder and lightning take turns scaring *the daylights out of me. I lean against the wall and slide down to the floor. Thirsty, I unhook the canteen from my belt and unscrew the top. Much to my disappointment, I realize I forgot to fill it with water. Angry, I toss it aside. As I watch it roll away, I get an idea. I pull my notepad and pen out of my pocket. I hold the flashlight between my lips and start writing.*

****

The sheriff's eyes fill with tears and blur his vision. His voice cracks as he finishes, "I just heard a bloodcurdling scream. It sounded like Jimmy. I'm afraid; but I can't hide in here forever. I think it is better to travel at night. I'm writing this note in case I don't make it. I'm going to stuff it in my canteen and leave it by the steps. I love you, Mom and Dad. Tell Grandma and Maggie I love them too. Jason Frazier."

Slamming his fist down on the desk, Sherriff James startles everyone in the room. Excitedly, he shouts, "I knew that son-of-a-bitch did it! I always knew it! I just couldn't prove it until now!"

The sheriff's outburst is followed by total silence. Everyone has tears in their eyes and lumps in their throats. Each person in the room has gotten a glimpse of the horror Jason and the other boys were forced to experience. It's hard to imagine the terror of being a child, lost and alone, waiting to be murdered. After the moment of truth passes, Sheriff James reaches across the desk and turns off the tape recorder. He and I light up cigarettes. Maggie cries softly. Then, she calms down and asks, "Has Jason given you what you need to get a warrant?"

Sheriff James focuses on Maggie. Frowning, he reports, "Yes, he has." He catches his breath and adds, "Jason was a very brave little boy. He would've made a great reporter."

Maggie looks up at the sheriff and smiles through her tears. In a prideful voice, she responds, "That was his dream. I guess he accomplished his goal." She catches her breath and adds, "I knew he wouldn't let the deacon get away with murder without putting up one Helluva of a fight."

The sheriff glances over at the deputy and stenographer. Reading his silent signal, both employees rise from their seats and head for the door. As they walk out of his office, the deputy whispers, "Good work, Sheriff."

Ready to right the wrong of sixteen years, Sheriff James states, "If I'm gonna arrest that perverted bastard, we've got to get him to set one foot in Watauga County."

Making eye contact with the sheriff, Maggie confides, "I have a plan in mind the good deacon won't be able to resist." Noting the look of concern in my eyes, she adds, "Trust me, I won't be in any danger."

Sheriff James responds, "Just tell me when and where?"

Concerned about the time frame, I interject, "You realize the State Bureau of Investigation is going to get involved?"

Sheriff James reports, "I can hold 'em off for about forty-eight hours after I've made the arrest; so, we better get our ducks in a row."

Maggie and I leave the sheriff's office and grab a bite to eat. When we return to our motel, a melancholy ambiance overshadows our success. Maggie and I go to our individual rooms. She takes the opportunity to call Carolyn and update her on our success. Afterwards, she takes a long, hot bath and goes to bed. I watch the local news. Around eleven, I crawl into bed. For the first time since I shook John's hand, I have a peaceful night's sleep.

Chapter 16

The Arrest

Maggie and I get up at daybreak on Sunday, May 18th. We hurriedly dress before starting our trek down the mountain. As we prepare to leave, the telephone rings. I pick up the receiver.

Hearing the sheriff's voice, I listen as he asks, "Are you and Maggie ready to go?"

I reply, "Yep, we're leaving in five minutes."

Anxious, Sheriff James requests, "Call me as soon as you know something."

After I reassure the sheriff everything is on go, I hang up the telephone. I turn to look at Maggie and inquire, "Are you ready?"

Nodding her pretty head, Maggie picks up her purse and heads out the door. We get in the car and drive southwest toward Asheville. As soon as we enter the city limits, I pull off the road into a restaurant parking lot. I get out and hold the door open. Maggie climbs out, walks around the car and gets into the driver's seat. I slam the door shut.

Leaning against the car, I ask, "Are you sure you want to do this alone?"

In a solemn tone, Maggie replies, "You know you can't come. If he sees you, John will get suspicious." As she puts the car in drive, Maggie adds, "I've been waiting all my life to settle the score for Jason. Trust me, I'll be just fine."

Maggie drives off. Within moments, she espies the church steeple. She pulls the car into the parking lot, finds an empty space and parks. She exits the car and walks into the sanctuary. After listening to Pastor Brown's sermon, she strolls out of the church along with other members of the congregation. Looking for the culprit, she mingles with the crowd. As soon as she spies him, Maggie makes her move. The determined young woman walks over to the big man, extends her hand and says, "I'm Maggie Harlow. I'm so happy to finally meet you. I've been trying to catch up with you for a couple of weeks now."

Addled, the deacon takes Maggie's hand. He introduces himself, saying, "I'm Deacon John Powers." Shaking her hand, he questions, "Why have you been looking for me?"

Maggie pulls her ID badge out of her purse. As she flashes her credentials, Maggie answers, "Here is my ID badge. I am a reporter for the Atlanta Journal. I'm on assignment here in North Carolina."

Deacon John scrutinizes her identification card. Puzzled, he questions, "What does any of this have to do with me?"

Maggie looks into the repulsive man's eyes and smiles demurely. Speaking in her rehearsed Southern accent, she drawls, "I'm interviewing people who have survived near-death experiences. I learned about your terrifying ordeal from some old newspaper clippings. I was so impressed by your story and religious affiliation I was compelled to seek you out."

Impressed by her striking beauty and interest in him, Deacon John grins from ear to ear. Curious, he questions, "What's your religion?"

Trying to create a common bond, Maggie returns his smile and confides, "I'm a devout Baptist. My soul was saved when I attended a Billy Graham crusade in Ohio. I was ten at the time. I thank God every day for His influence in my life."

The beautiful, young reporter bedazzles the deacon. Lowering his head in modesty, Deacon John blushes and says, "Amen! But I really don't think my story is worthy of your time and attention."

Maggie waves her finger under his nose and protests, "I'm the journalist here. I know what kind of stories interest my readers." In an effort to heighten his interest, she stops and catches her breath before continuing, "Why do you think the newspaper pays for human interest stories?"

Deacon John's curiosity is piqued by the mention of money. Giving the young reporter his undivided attention, he inquires, "How much money?"

Maggie bats her eyes and lies, "The paper pays all expenses for time and travel. If your story is selected for print, the publisher will pay you up to ten thousand dollars for publishing rights."

The deacon is delighted by the prospect of fame and fortune. He exclaims, "You are saying, if I give you permission to write about what happened to me sixteen years ago, your newspaper will pay me ten thousand dollars?"

Maggie not only holds the bait she taunts her prey with it. Looking directly into John's eyes, she responds, "Yes, but I don't want to compromise your ethics. If you are uncomfortable with my offer, I'm certain I can find another local survivor to take your place."

The big man raises his arms in surrender. Smiling broadly, he asks, "When and where do you want to conduct your interview?"

Catching her breath, Maggie provides the deacon with the details. They shake hands to seal the deal. Several members of the congregation approach, wanting his attention. Maggie takes the opportunity to steal away. She scurries back to the car and speeds out of the parking lot. As soon as she picks me up, we head back to Boone. When we got back to our motel, I call Sheriff James and advise him of the plan. After I hang up the telephone, I notice Maggie is trembling. Overwhelmed with anger and excitement, she admits, "The next twenty-four hours is going to seem like an eternity. I wish I could fast forward time. But much to my chagrin, I used all my charm setting the trap."

******

Monday, May 19th, Maggie stands on the porch of the Daniel Boone Inn. She glances nervously at her watch and sees both hands pointing at one. Sheriff James and his deputy sit in their police car, waiting for John to show. I occupy a seat in the lobby, facing the entrance. Staring into the distance, Maggie hears a man's voice close to her ear. Startled, she turns and gulps for air as John says, "Miss Harlow, I hope I haven't kept you waiting?"

Maggie looks up into the face of this ordinary looking man. She gazes into his dark beady eyes as they peer through horn-rimmed glasses. She thinks, *there is nothing about this man's appearance that singles him out in a crowd. His demeanor isn't the least bit intimidating.* As the deacon waits for her response, Maggie is lost in thought, thinking, *how can such an unexceptional person cause so much pain and misery and never get caught?*

John touches her arm and repeats, "I hope I haven't kept you waiting?"

Maggie doesn't say a word. She looks behind him and watches the sheriff and deputy approach. When they are within hearing distance, she looks up at John and says, "As a matter of fact, you've kept me waiting for sixteen years. At last, my wait is over."

Confused the deacon responds, "I beg your pardon. Don't you mean minutes?"

Maggie ignores his question and steps aside for the two officers. She smiles smugly and announces, "John Powers, I'd like to introduce you to Sheriff James and Deputy Cunningham."

Surprised but not the least bit intimidated, John extends his arm to shake hands with the two officers. With his arm outstretched, the sheriff fastens handcuffs on his wrist. Before his suspect can speak or react, Sheriff James declares, "John Wesley Powers, I'm placing you under arrest for the murders of Jason Frazier, Jimmy Simmons, Rusty Campbell, Steve Douglas and Charlie Reynolds." As John stands dumbfounded, Sheriff James glares at him and orders, "Deputy Cunningham, recite the Miranda to the prisoner."

Before the deputy has a chance to speak, John shrugs his shoulders and exclaims, "Don't bother!" Ignoring his remark, the officer quotes the Miranda. The churchman vehemently protests, "You're making a grave mistake! I've come here to be interviewed by this reporter. She represents the national press! I would think twice before I embarrassed my city and state by making these ridiculous and unsubstantiated charges!"

As tears cascade down her cheeks, Maggie looks fiercely at the deacon. With rabid hatred in her eyes, she shrieks, "You are the one who is mistaken! I'm the childhood sweetheart of Jason Frazier! He was one of the boys you brutally murdered on August 21, 1987! And I've come a long way to see you in handcuffs!" Getting more emotional, she gasps, "It's true! I am a journalist! But, the story I intend to write is the one which reports you being found guilty of murder! And, I pray you get the death penalty!"

Maggie stands rigid as she watches the sheriff and deputy escort the deacon to their patrol car and guide him into the backseat. While tears stream down her face, I approach from behind. Sensing my presence, Maggie gasps, "Did you see the sheriff arrest that bastard?"

I answer, "Yeah, but we really need John to confess in order to spare everyone the heartache of a long, messy trial." I take a deep breath and add, "I'm making it my business to get his confession."

******

Maggie and I head straightway to the police station. Not wanting to expose my hand, we wait in the car while John is led into the building. After an ample amount of time has passed, we go inside and make a beeline for the sheriff's office. In a few minutes, Sheriff James bolts through the door. He reports, "We are putting John through processing. He hasn't asked for a lawyer. The later it gets, the longer it'll take one to get here."

I retrieve one of my cigarettes and light it. Looking at the sheriff, I ask, "How much time do we have before the state boys get involved?"

Glancing at his watch, Sheriff James responds, "About twelve hours. Tomorrow morning, this entire case will be out of my hands."

I glance at the beautiful, young woman who managed to lure the fly into our web. Noting the dark circles under her eyes, I speak directly to the sheriff and confide, "Maggie didn't get much sleep last night. I'm going to take her to the motel. I'll take a short nap myself and get back down here around midnight. If the deacon hasn't confessed by then, I'd like to take a stab at him."

Sheriff James coughs as though something is lodged in his throat. Catching his breath, he quips, "Was that a play on words or a death threat?"

I stand and glare at the sheriff. Not finding his remark the least bit amusing, I retort, "I didn't help you catch him to kill him. I could've done that on my own time."

Grinning, Sheriff James jokes, "I was just playing with you." After taking a few moments to consider my offer, the sheriff proposes, "I'll keep at John until midnight. You can take it from there. If we don't get a confession, it will be up to the state to prosecute him."

******

Maggie and I leave the police station and return to the motel. We eat a snack in the café. Emotionally and physically drained, we are both lost in our own thoughts. Needing some privacy, Maggie goes to her room. I opt for a drink at the bar.

After taking a hot bath, Maggie picks up the telephone and calls Carolyn. As soon as she hears a voice on the line, Maggie exclaims, "We've done it! I lured Deacon John into Boone! The sheriff arrested him! The bastard is being processed as we speak!" After Carolyn lets out a joyful cry, Maggie explains, "Boone is too small a town to handle such a high profile case. So, the State Bureau of Investigation will take him into custody tomorrow. John will be arraigned in Raleigh or Charlotte. I'm not sure which but I'll keep you posted."

Carolyn exclaims, "That's wonderful news! Tom would be so proud of you!" As she chokes back tears, she asks, "What are your plans?"

Maggie is jolted back to reality by Carolyn's question. She stops and catches her breath. Reflecting on her present circumstances, she is silent for a few moments. Carolyn waits patiently for a response. Talking in a slow and deliberate manner, Maggie confides, "It could take a year or more for the case to go to trial. If John is found guilty, he could get the death penalty. There is no telling how long it will take to execute him. But, I'll follow the case from start to finish."

Maggie hangs up the phone and lies down on the bed. Being totally focused on gathering evidence and seeing John behind bars, it didn't occur to her that we might be going in separate directions. When her eyes close and she falls asleep, I am foremost in her thoughts.

I am experiencing my own dilemma. My sentiments are bittersweet. I'm happy and relieved John has been arrested. But, my job isn't done. I'm obligated to keep my promise to Betsy Bond. I'm not going to accept a guilty verdict for the murders of five boys as full payment for all crimes committed. Until the whole truth is exposed, I'm determined to continue my investigation of John's shadowy past. After downing a few drinks in the hotel bar, I return to my room and change into sweats. I watch television for a couple of hours. About nine, I turn off the tube and overhead light. Leaving on the bedside lamp, I set the clock and stretch out on the bed. Eventually, I drift off to sleep.

******

During my dream state, a celestial being approaches me. As the figure draws near, I recognize my guardian Angel. I feel humble and awed by the Heavenly presence amidst the ethereal surroundings. The Angel takes my hand and leads me into an assembly hall where five council members sit at a long table. The gathering place is alive with shimmering white lights and pulsating energy. Speaking in unison, the five spiritual advisers welcome me, saying, "We've called you before us in response to prayers for lost souls. Your mission is to rescue them from limbo." *As I stand silent and in awe, the five voices explain, "There are three souls who are haunting the earth as a result of being murdered by the man who calls himself, John Wesley Powers. In order for these ghosts to accept their deaths, their bodies must be found and given a proper burial. You will need divine intervention to accomplish this goal. For this specific reason, you're going to view a screening of the life history of the murderer. Answers will be revealed which will enable you to elicit a confession."*

Standing erect, I listen intently to the Divine Council's words. From experience, I know there is a catch .. I wait to hear it. The five voices read my mind and continue, "There is one condition attached to this mission of mercy. After you use your sacred insight, this knowledge will be forever erased from your memory. Do you understand, Jason?"

When the council calls me, Jason, I'm dumbfounded! I step backwards to catch my breath and find myself outside the gathering place. Instantaneously, my Angelic guide spreads its crystal wings and reveals a panoramic viewing on the life of the man posing as John Wesley Powers.

******

I awaken from my dream and look at the clock. The hands indicate the midnight hour. I get up, go into the bathroom to shower. I dress in casual attire and head out the door.

Chapter 17

The Confession

I walk into the office and find Sheriff James sitting at his desk. Frowning, he looks up and advises, "John hasn't asked for an attorney. He's so pompous he doesn't think he needs legal counsel." The officer of the law pauses to light a cigarette. Inhaling the smoke into his lungs, he continues, "He isn't admitting to anything. He claims the assailants buried his jacket, eyeglasses and knife. He says Jason's note is a forgery. John actually accused me of writing it to frame him. He said I'm trying to make him the sacrificial lamb."

As the sheriff rises to leave, I remark, "You look exhausted. Why don't you go home and let me take it from here."

As his eyes reflect his disappointment, Sheriff James replies, "I wanted to turn John over to the state boys wrapped in a neat little package." Adopting a more positive attitude, he pats me on the back and states, "You'll have the interrogation room to yourselves. Make the prisoner aware you're recording your interrogation. If you manage to convince John to confess, have him write his confession on the yellow pad I left on the table. Make certain he signs and dates it."

Waiting a moment to be certain the sheriff is finished with his instructions, I nod my head and respond, "Get a good night's sleep. You've earned it."

As he walks out of his office, Sheriff James looks down the hall and sees an officer sitting at the desk. He calls out, "Jim, take Zack to the interrogation room and bring in the prisoner!"

I follow the deputy to the designated area. I lean against the wall and wait for John. In a matter of minutes, the oversized man is led into the room. At first, he is startled to see me. After the shock factor diminishes, he smiles smugly, takes a seat and acts nonchalant about his predicament.

The deputy inquires, "Do you want me to remove his handcuffs or leave them on?" I motion for him to remove them. After taking off the metal restraints, the deputy glares at John as he prepares to leave the room. He adjusts his belt and holster as he states, "I'll be right outside. Knock on the door if you need me."

As soon as the officer leaves us alone, I sit down at the far end of the table, remove a pack of cigarettes from my jacket pocket and offer one to the churchman. John waves off my friendly gesture. I light a cigarette and inhale deeply. Blowing smoke rings into the air, I don't say anything.

Leering at me, John snarls, "I should've known you were behind these false charges. I could see the contempt in your eyes when you came into my store. It made no difference to you I was genuinely concerned and tried to help you when you got sick." The big man hesitates before adding, "Now, I'm being rewarded for my compassion by being held prisoner in this one-horse town."

I glare at the deacon and counter, "Did you ever think the very sight of you might have caused me to get sick to my stomach?" I inhale on my cigarette, exhale and hiss, "I'm not the reason you're in jail charged with five counts of murder. You're the one who stabbed five young boys to death and walked away pretending to be a victim."

John retaliates, "How dare you sit in judgment of me! You know nothing about me!"

I make eye contact with the deacon. My rage is surfacing. I'm fighting to control my temper. In a husky voice, I declare, "That's where you're dead wrong! I know every detail of your life. And, I know you murdered eight people not five."

Stunned by my words, John stares into my icy cold eyes. He challenges my hostility and shouts, "You're completely insane or …!"

I throw down my cigarette, jump out of my seat and grab the suspect by the neck! I pull him out of his seat and lift him so high in the air his feet dangle like a puppet on a string! His face turns beet red as he eyes bulge out of their sockets due to the pressure I'm applying to his throat! Several seconds hang in the balance before I realize I'm holding the big man in mid air without straining a muscle! Shocked by my superhuman strength, I release my grip! John falls to the floor! He is stupefied! The only thing he finds more frightening than my physical prowess is the raging hatred in my eyes! The color drains from his face. Without taking his eyes off me, the cowardly giant hunches down and crawls back to his chair. At the same moment, I sit down and act as though nothing out of the ordinary has taken place.

Several moments pass before John dares to speak. He whispers, "Who are you? How do you know me? What do you want?"

I retort, "First and foremost, I know you are not John Wesley Powers. That individual was born in May of fifty-three and died in June of fifty-five. You got a copy of his birth certificate in sixty-nine and used that document to assume your new identity."

Smiling maliciously, John challenges, "Any good detective could've got hold of that information. I'm not impressed."

I get out of my chair and walk around the room. I stop and lean against the wall behind the accused. Suspicious of my tactics, John turns and faces me. Grinning, I quip, "Good, because I've just begun." With deliberate control, I light another cigarette and reveal, "You were born in the spring of fifty-three. Your given name is Henry. Your family lived in a cabin deep in the Appalachian Mountains. Your father made his money selling moonshine. Every Saturday night, he'd get drunk off his own brew."

Hearing Zack's words in the background, John relives the events in his mind:

John is a small boy for his twelve years. He is crying as he watches his dad beat his mother. Then, he cringes in fear when the big man pushes her aside and turns to look at him. John screams for help as his father approaches. He fights back but is helpless against the brute strength. His father lifts John out of his hiding place and carries him from the house into the barn. He ties the boy to a pole as John begs for mercy. Then, the drunk reaches for a riding crop and starts beating his son. Large whelps form on his skin as the boy screams in pain. This form of physical abuse sexually arouses the father figure. He starts to molest John and everything goes black.

I pause and search John's eyes for denial. Seeing and hearing no contradiction, I continue talking. The terrifying visions float back into his head as he remembers:

John's father lays passed out on the straw. The youngster manages to untie his hands. He picks up a shovel and uses all his strength to hit his dad over the head. Blood gushes from the wound and little John runs from the wooden building in terror. His mother hears his screams, comes out of the house and sprints into the barn. She sees her husband lying in a pool of blood. She runs back to the house to get medical supplies. She stops in her tracks when she sees her son standing alone and crying. She grabs John by the arms and orders him to get as far away as possible. She tells him to never come back home. John kisses and hugs his mother. Then, he turns and runs into the darkness ...

Coming out of his reverie, tears run down his face. Consciously, John hears me say, "You followed your mother's orders. You never knew if your father lived or died."

John argues, "You could've found that out by nosing into my past."

Undaunted, I puff on my cigarette and shrug my shoulders. Exhaling, I continue, "You wound up in Atlanta and found shelter in the basement of a Baptist church. The youth minister befriended you. You listened to his preaching and did odd jobs to sustain yourself. In time, you made friends with two other runaways. Alice taught you to read and write. Mickey educated you on the art of survival." I stop talking and extinguish my cigarette in the ashtray. Then, I go on, "At eighteen, you joined the Army. Going against the odds, you made sexual advances toward another soldier. He reported you to the Captain, forcing you to resign from duty."

John is enraged at being reminded of his sordid past. He gets red-faced with anger. Without thinking, he exclaims, "Those charges were bogus! The Army could never have proven its case! Eddie would never have had the balls to testify against ..." John stops talking in mid sentence. Suddenly, it occurs to him, he is admitting his guilt by denying the accusations. Now, his curiosity is really piqued. He loudly demands, "Who allowed you access to my personal history?"

Knowing the truth is more frightening than fiction, I reveal, "My soul was brought before a Heavenly Council and shown your life experiences from birth to the present."

Confident my explanation will astound and frighten the deacon to an even greater extent, I hush and allow silence to work in my behalf. Hoping for a glimpse of deception, John studies my eyes. When he accepts the fact I believe what I'm saying, he sits dumbfounded. Trying to downplay his concern, John scoffs, "You're kidding, right? Why you? What makes you so special?"

I cross the room and stand next to John. I lean forward and down. I get so close to him our noses almost touch. Daring him to face his past, I ask, "Don't you recognize me?" Avoiding my eyes, he sits motionless in his chair and ignores my question. I wait for some show of emotion. Getting none, I lean forward until the heat of my breath tickles his ear. Whispering, I confide, "My soul was originally born into the body of Jason Frazier. Sixteen years ago, you murdered my body but not my soul. My spirit refused to accept its fate and returned to haunt the Earth."

Giving my killer time to digest what I'm saying, I stand upright and flick my ashes into the ashtray.

Stupefied, John hardly dares to breathe. He is paralyzed with fear. When his natural reflexes kick in, he gasps for air. Rocking back and forth in his chair, he hangs his head low and wrings his hands. I sit down on the table and stare down at the terrified and confused man.

After giving him a few seconds to rebound, I explain, "Six years ago, Zack Lee was involved in a serious car accident. His soul entered the dead zone and was lifted up into Heaven. It wasn't his time to die. His soul was told to return to its physical body. Zack didn't want to go back and begged for mercy." I take a final puff on my cigarette and extinguish it in the ashtray. Talking slowly, I enunciate, "My spirit was waiting in the ethers. It was ready and eager to possess a strong, virile body. After pleading our cases, a soul exchange was sanctioned by the Heavenly Council. Zack's spirit remained in Heaven. My soul returned to Earth with a vengeance and took possession of Zack's body. From the moment I inhaled my first breath of life as Zack, my primary goal has been to hunt you down and bring you to justice."

Hunching low in his seat and trembling uncontrollably, John is mortified. Speaking in a whisper, he contests, "I believe all souls go straight to Heaven or Hell. I don't think they have any choice in the matter."

I jump up and walk the length of the table before turning around. Pounding my fist on the table for effect, I hiss, 'I'm not here to explain the afterlife to you! My purpose is to settle our debt!"

My propensity for violence keeps John prone. Daring to look at me, he is shocked to see my face transform into the image of young Jason. Spellbound by the vision, he convulses until my features return to normal. Experiencing heart palpitations, my murderer gasps, "What do you want from me?"

I pull a copy of my handwritten note out of my pocket. I put the document down on the table and order, "I want you to read this letter. Then, I want you to validate its contents by signing and dating it."

John asks, "Don't you want me to write down what happened?"

Frowning, I reply, "I have re-lived the murder scene way too many times already. You know what happened. I know what happened. This letter describes what happened. Enough is enough."

John picks up the letter. I hand him a pen. He takes it. He starts to read. I stop him. I lean over and turn on the tape recorder. Then, I order, "Read as you write."

John clears his throat and begins. After he has read what Jason wrote, he concludes, "This letter is a true and accurate account of what happened on the night of August 21, 1987. I murdered five boys. Their given names were Rusty, Steve, Charlie, Jimmy, and Jason … signed John Wesley Powers … May 19, 2003."

I reach over and turn off the recorder, remove

the tape, grab the signed confessions and walk out of the room. I hand the paper and tape to the deputy. As he looks at me, I report, "Here's John's confession for the first five murders. Make copies and put the original in a safe place." As I head down the hall, I add, "I need to take a break. I'll be back in a few minutes and find out about Billy Bond."

I continue walking and exit the building. Needing physical support, I lean against the lamppost. My blood pressure is going up and down like a roller coaster. I spend several minutes breathing in the fresh air. Counteracting the cleansing process, I chain-smoke three cigarettes. I throw the last butt down on the sidewalk and extinguish it with my foot. At last, I'm ready to face my killer again and extract the truth about Billy. I walk back inside the station and retrieve another tape. Then, I pour two cups of coffee and carry them into the interrogation room. While John sits staring into space, I place a cup of the hot brew on the table in front of him. Afterwards, I sit down opposite my murderer. I knock on the table to bring the deacon out of his stupor and announce, "It's time to talk about Billy."

John glances up at me, looks back down at his hands and begins to cry. He sobs, "Where do I begin?"

As I hand him the yellow pad and pen, I suggest, "At the beginning."

Waiting for John to speak, I light a cigarette, put the tape in the recorder, hit the start button and ask, "Is it okay if I record your confession?"

John takes a drink of coffee and nods his head. I state, "I need a verbal reply."

John responds, "Yes, you have my permission to record this statement which I make of my own free will." He stops talking, takes off his eyeglasses and cleans them with his shirt. Taking a few seconds to organize his thoughts, the prisoner begins, "After the campsite murders, I tried to forget what I'd done. I rededicated my life to God. I kept my relationships outside the church until I met Billy. I was so smitten with him I bribed him to join my study group by tempting him with good food, great friends and social outings." The big man chokes and brings his hand up to his mouth. After coughing several times, he continues, "Billy reminded me of myself as a child. He was lanky, impoverished and a social misfit. His mother loved him but she couldn't give him what he needed, a father figure."

Tears spurt out of the deacon's eyes and run down his cheeks. He wipes his face with the back of his hand. Unsympathetic and repulsed by his very presence, I urge, "Get on with it."

Speaking in a shallow voice, John confides, "I was never a powerful man. I never had any great influence over people or events. I've spent my life living in the shadow of others."

I interrupt, "Save the sob story for the jury."

Ignoring my remark, John swallows hard to dislodge the lump in his throat. In a husky voice, he continues, "Billy captured my heart. He didn't know his own father. And, I wanted to whitewash the shame of being born a bastard. I bought him gifts; but he refused to take them. I offered him money; but he threw it in my face. I tried every way I knew to win his affection but Billy wasn't interested in sharing my love."

I pull my chair closer and stare intently at the large man. Speaking in a low voice, I probe, "What happened the night Billy went missing?"

John takes a deep breath, exhales slowly and recalls, "As soon as his mother dropped him off at the church, Billy came into my office. He told me it was the last time he was coming to Bible class. I asked why? He wouldn't look at me and kept fidgeting. Finally, he said I made him nervous." The weeping man takes a deep breath and goes on, "I was heartbroken. I pleaded with Billy to think about his decision. But, he puckered up his lips and whined, 'I ain't coming back and you know why.'"

John stops talking and takes a drink of coffee. Staring into his cup, he continues, "Bart and Larry barged into the office and interrupted our conversation. Since it was time for class, I had to forget about Billy and take care of business. An hour or so later, I took the boys to the movie." His chin quivers as he admits, "During the movie, I got sexually aroused. Without thinking, I reached over and put my hand on Billy's privates. He got mad as Hell! He grabbed my hand and jerked it away! Then, he jumped up and punched me as hard as he could! After that, he ran out of the theatre."

The deacon gets quiet and stares into space. I lean closer and persist, "What did you do next?"

John lets out a long, deep, audible breath. He replies, "I stayed with the other two boys and watched the rest of the movie. When Billy didn't come back, we spent fifteen or twenty minutes looking for him inside and outside the theatre. It was getting late. I knew the other boys' parents were waiting to pick them up; so, I drove them back to the church."

Not wanting to say the words out loud, John stops talking. He looks up and sees the expression on my face. Terrified of another confrontation, he picks up where he left off, confiding, "I always took Billy home after our socials; so I knew what route he would take. I set out to find him." He starts sweating profusely. Beads of perspiration appear on his forehead. He shuffles in his seat. Nervously, he admits, "I saw Billy on the side of the road and pulled up beside him. I rolled down my window and ordered him to get in the car. He screamed, 'No way, you *sick-o!*' Then, he took off running.

John hesitates and takes a deep breath. His voice raises two octaves as he confesses, "I threw the car in park, jumped out and chased the boy! I caught him and grabbed him by the arm! He fought back! I backhanded him! I heard a popping sound and Billy collapsed! I ordered him to get up; but he didn't move! I nudged him with my shoe. He still didn't move! I bent down and checked his vital signs! There weren't any! Billy was dead! I didn't know what to do?" The pedophile hushes for a moment and glances over at me. Seeing no sign of sympathy, he exclaims, "I panicked! I checked for witnesses! I didn't see anybody; so, I picked Billy up and carried him to my car.! I put his body in the backseat, jumped in and took off like a bat out of Hell!"

As his words reverberate in the small room, the atmosphere becomes chilly and eerily quiet. Although my killer is sitting in a chair crying like a baby, the sound of his sobs are lost to me as Billy's fate is finally exposed. Everything comes to a standstill … the truth hangs suspended in the ethereal *NOW*.

Suddenly, my bodily functions jolt me back to reality. I fight the urge to regurgitate. I want to cry and laugh at the same time. Cry from the pain … anguish … horror … inflicted by child predators. Cry for every individual, living or dead, who has the misfortune of coming in contact with this type of sick, perverted monster. Laugh because the good guy has finally caught the killer in his own web of deception. But in the midst of it all, I'm relieved this cycle of death and perversion ends here and now. When the heat from the butt of my cigarette burns my fingertips, I'm startled back to reality. I react by putting out one cigarette and lighting another. I inhale deeply, exhale and blow smoke into John's face. Finding my voice, I ask, "How did you dispose of the body?"

John snaps out of his stupor and retorts, "I didn't

dispose of the body! I gave Billy a proper burial."

I pry, "Where?"

Mentally and physically exhausted, the prisoner responds, "I have property in the mountains, northeast of Asheville. I buried him there."

Certain Billy isn't out there alone, I rise to my feet. I toss the notepad on the table and walk over to John. As I look down at him, he avoids my eyes. I kick his foot to get his undivided attention. John reacts by glancing up at me. I take the opportunity to look deep into his soul. Sounding deep and hoarse, I inquire, "Is Billy the only person buried out there?"

Refusing to keep eye contact, John looks away. He coughs and covers his mouth with his hand. Although his words are muffled, I hear, "No, there are two more."

I ball my fists. I'd like nothing better than to beat the Hell out of the perverted bastard. But, because of my training as an officer of the law, I realize it's critical at this phase of the investigation to keep my cool. Taking a deep breath, I unclench my fists and ask, "Who?"

John heaves a sigh and answers, "Lone Wolf and a runaway." Not waiting for me to ask why, he blurts out, "Lone Wolf caught me having sex with the boy! He went ballistic! We fought! I killed him with my bare hands!"

Ashen, I shake my head, take a step backward and heave a sigh of dismay. In a tired voice, I ask, "Did he go into a jealous rage?"

John laughs maliciously before he answers, "Not hardly! Lone Wolf was as straight as an arrow! He was mad as Hell that I was molesting a child!"

I already know the answer to my next question before I ask, "What about the child?"

John lets out a loud sob as tears roll down his cheeks. He gasps, "I had to kill him. He saw me strangle Lone Wolf. There was no way I could let him live and tell people what he saw.

I only have one more matter to deal with before I can leave. In a calm voice, I inquire, "Will you show the authorities where the bodies are buried?"

Realizing he still has a small degree of leverage, John grins as he retorts, "If you and the pretty lady reporter come along?"

Puffing on my cigarette, I walk away from the deacon. I take another hit before I put it out in the ashtray. With my back to the accused, I inquire, "Why do you want her to come?"

Straightening his posture, John responds, "She came to North Carolina looking for a story. I thought I'd give her what she wants."

Knowing Maggie will demand to see this case to

the end, I nod my head in agreement. Then, I hand John the yellow notepad and a pen. I order, "Now, put everything you just told me in writing. Sign and date it."

As he writes, I turn off the recorder and remove the tape. When the prisoner finishes writing, signs his name and records the date, I take the pad and pen. Without uttering a single word, I exit the room, hand everything to the deputy and head down the hall. As soon as I enter the lobby, I pick up the phone and call the sheriff. When he answers, I say, "I'm sorry to wake you but I want you to know John confessed. He has admitted to the campsite murders in addition to killing three other people, including Billy Bond. I gave your deputy his signed confession along with a tape recording of the details."

Sheriff James shouts, "No shit! We need to celebrate!" Hearing no hint of jubilation in my voice, he shifts gears and says, "I hate to hear more people were murdered but I'm relieved a trial won't be necessary." Sensing an undertone in my voice, he asks, "Are you okay?"

I reply, "I'm fine. I'm just not myself tonight." After a brief silence, I advise, "John claims he buried the bodies on his property. He has agreed to show the authorities where if Maggie and I tag along." I catch my breath and direct, "You need to call the State Bureau of Investigation and make them aware of the condition."

Sheriff James reports, "I'm dressing now. I'll put

in a call as soon as I get to the office." He pauses and asks, "What are you going to do?"

I look at my watch and answer, "It's after two. I'm going back to my hotel and grab a few hours of sleep. Maggie and I will be here first thing in the morning."

Chapter 18

Recovery

I roll over in bed, open my eyes and glance at the clock. Startled to see it is six-thirty, I jump up and grab the phone! I dial the sheriff's office and wait for an answer. As soon as I hear his voice, I'm sorry! I overslept! I can be there in fifteen minutes!"

Confused, Sheriff James asks, "What are you talking about? You just left here a little while ago."

My head starts spinning. I turn on the light. I'm shocked to see I'm dressed. Totally disoriented, I take a deep breath and try to figure out what is going on. Stalling for time and answers, I ask, "How long was I there?"

The sheriff raises his voice an octave and inquires, "Is this some kind of joke?"

I respond, "No, I just woke up. I'm a little groggy." Dumbfounded, I wrack my brain for answers. Somewhere in the recesses of my mind, I recall, *I dreamt I went to the station. The sheriff is saying I was actually there.*

Was I dreaming or not? Talking in a normal tone, I pry, "Refresh my memory?"

Somewhat addled, the sheriff recalls, "You got here about one. We had a short chat. I left. Dave took you to the interrogation room. Around one thirty, you came out carrying John's confession to the campsite murders. You took a short break, went back in and stayed until the old boy confessed to killing Billy, Lone Wolf and another boy."

I can't believe what I'm hearing. I know the sheriff has no reason to lie. Needing more information, I probe, "You and Dave both saw me, right?"

Sheriff James retorts, "Damn straight."

Suddenly it dawns on me, *If I wasn't dreaming and I managed to get John's confession, I'd be a fool to say anything to the contrary.* I take a few moments to organize my thoughts. Having no logical explanation for my lapse in memory, I decide to keep my mouth shut. The sheriff clears his throat to get my attention. Grasping at straws, I bluff, "Why aren't we out celebrating?"

In a glib voice, the sheriff exclaims, "That's the same question I asked you but you said you weren't yourself. I just assumed you were too damn tired to tie one on."

Hoping I sound convincing, I reply, "Sad but true. This case must be aging me because my memory is not up to par."

My mental status is not the sheriff's concern. He

222

is too excited about the confession. He exclaims, "There's no way in Hell John will slip through the crack this time!"

As I listen to the sheriff's words, I wrack my brain for answers. I try to visualize what might have occurred earlier in the evening. I form a mental image of the police station. I see myself walk into the interrogation room. I look for John. Working on overload, my imagination brings the tape recorder into focus. Hoping for a tangible clue of the night's events, I inquire, "Did I get John's confession on tape?"

Sheriff James takes a deep breath and replies, "Yep, but the tape where John confesses to murdering Jason and the other boys is full of static. The only part that is audible is when John reads Jason's letter and verifies that it is a true and accurate report of what happened. Thank God, this is all we need to convict him of the campsite murders." As I remain quiet, the sheriff continues, "The second tape recorded all the details of why and how he killed Billy, Lone Wolf and another boy."

Continuing to push the envelope, I ask, "Did I get his confessions in writing?"

The sheriff responds, "Yep, his confessions are signed, sealed and delivered." Getting a little irritated, he quizzes, "What's wrong with you? Don't you remember anything?

I think, *You don't know the half of it.* Lying, I answer, "I've lost so much sleep lately I must've been running on automatic pilot." I catch my breath and grab an idea out of thin air. Reacting to it, I exclaim, "This case would never have been solved if it weren't for Maggie. I think she has a right to hear John's confession with her own ears."

Sheriff James is quiet while he contemplates my suggestion. Then, he agrees, "You're absolutely right! Get here as soon as you can. I'll give you two a listen."

More than ready to get off the phone, I respond, " Maggie and I will be there ASAP."

The telephone goes dead. I sit on the bed and try to recall going to the sheriff's office. For the life of me, I can't remember getting out of bed much less John confessing. My mind is blank. I go into Maggie's room and wake her. I make her aware of the circumstances. The two of us get dressed as fast as possible and head to the sheriff's office.

******

On Tuesday morning, May 20th, at eight o'clock sharp, I park in front of the police station. Sheriff James is standing in the parking lot, waiting for Maggie and me. As soon as we approach, he confides, "When I left here last night, I had no hope of getting a confession. I thought John was far too pompous to admit to a parking ticket much less murder." He focuses on me, smiles and exclaims, "I don't know how you did it but congratulations are in order! Thanks to you, John Powers is guilty by his own admission!"

Maggie gasps, "I can hardly believe it myself."

Sheriff James watches several cars pass by the building. Then, he glances at us and offers, "I left the tape in the recorder on my desk. Hurry in there and listen. I keep the state boys busy until you're finished."

Maggie and I head into his office. When she sits down, I turn on the recorder. We listen to the first tape and hear John confess to murdering Billy, Lone Wolf and the other boy. When it stops, I put the other tape in the machine. As reported by the sheriff, the bulk of the tape is nothing but static. The only part that is audible is when John reads Jason's letter and validates its contents. After I turn off the recorder, Maggie looks at me and asks, "What caused all that static?"

I shake my head and respond, "I don't have a clue." I think to myself, *she has no idea how true my words are.* There is a knock on the door. Deputy Matthews sticks his head inside and reports, "The state boys are here. Sheriff James wants you two to come outside and meet them."

Maggie and I follow the deputy outside. Introductions are exchanged. Turning his attention to me, Agent Hughes says, "I understand the prisoner refuses to lead us to the bodies unless you and Miss Harlow are present?"

Returning his gaze, I state, "I was hired by Ms. Betsy Bond to find her missing son, Billy. John has admitted he is one of his victims. I am committed to follow my investigation until I find Billy or his body."

Agent Reilly looks at Maggie and asks, "What about you, Miss Harlow?'

Maggie responds, "Please call me Maggie." Sighing, she explains, "I have a vested interest in this case. My childhood sweetheart was one of the victims. I have helped Sheriff James and Zack with this investigation. I think I've earned the right to see it to the end."

Nodding his head, Agent Hughes advises, "We will take John with us. You two will have to follow in your own vehicle." He looks at his watch, checks the time and continues, "It will take several hours to reach the location. State troopers equipped with the proper gear will meet us en route."

Talking to the sheriff, Agent Reilly confides, "We will handle John with kid gloves until we know where the bodies are buried. At that point, he becomes just another prisoner and won't get special treatment 'cause he's a church deacon." Looking from Maggie to me, he draws a deep breath before asking, "Do either of you have a problem with that?"

I say, "I'm here to find Billy. How you treat the prisoner is your own business."

Maggie chimes in, "I could care less." She catches her breath and continues, "At this stage of the game, my only purpose is to expose the deacon to the public. And, I have every intention of witnessing his execution."

Agent Hughes confirms, "We're all on the same page then." He turns to face the sheriff and inquires, "Are you coming with us?"

Shaking his head, Sheriff James replies, "Nope, my job stops in Boone. Thanks to this fine young couple, I can retire knowing the campsite killer has been caught." Grinning with pride, he adds, "I'm more than ready for y'all to take him off my hands."

Everyone hushes as two deputies approach with John in tow. We stand aside as the agents shackle his wrists and ankles. In a stern voice, the larger man states, "John Wesley Powers, I'm Agent Reilly. This is Agent Hughes. We are with the State Bureau of Investigation. We were summoned by Sheriff James to take you to Asheville." He looks at John and inquires, "It is our understanding you have agreed to show us where you have buried three missing persons?"

John avoids the agent's eyes, looks at me and announces, "I have no qualms about making a stand. If Jason goes, I go. If not, I won't show you boys anything but the back of my head."

Caught completely off guard, Agent Hughes asks, "Who is Jason?"

John doesn't answer the agent. Instead, he looks at me and says, "You tell him, Jason."

Utterly dumbfounded, I look at John and argue, "What is wrong with you? You know full well who I am!" I take a deep breath and add, "Maggie and I have agreed to your condition only because we want your victims identified and given a proper burial."

As the two agents move to take him in tow, John becomes fearful and whines, "Ride with me, Jason."

I ignore his plea. Agent Hughes steps between us. Confronting the prisoner, he advises, "Detective Lee isn't an employee of the bureau. He can't ride in a government vehicle."

John doesn't say anything to the officer. He simply winks at me as though we share a special secret. Maggie is obviously disturbed by John referring to me as Jason. Looking to me for answers, she asks, "What is he talking about?"

Shaking my head, I respond, "Apparently, John is acting crazy in a last ditch effort to cop a plea." Maggie continues to stare at me. Feeling most uncomfortable, I persist, "I don't have a clue what he's talking about. I'm just buying time until I can tell him what I really think."

In an effort to skirt the issue, I watch the two agents flank John and escort him to their car. Sheriff James approaches me and shakes my hand. Both of us are consciously aware we share a special bond that will survive time. After we've said our goodbyes, Maggie smiles up at the sheriff and pecks him on the cheek. Then, the two of us head for my car. We climb inside and I pull into position behind the agents.

En route to Asheville, three state patrol cars join

the caravan and trek through the mountains. At the proper junction, the lead car turns off the rural highway onto a secondary road. Houses can be seen in the distance overlooking the countryside. The rustic homes become sparse as we head deeper into the woods. After another five miles or so, we turn left onto a gravel road and travel at a snail's pace up the incline. The lead car stops at a swing gate. Agent Hughes gets out, removes the padlock and chain, pulls the metal barrier open and climbs back into his car. Each vehicle inches through the narrow passageway and comes to a halt in front of a crudely built cabin. Everyone gets out of their vehicles, including the six troopers who have joined the entourage. The new recruits remove shovels from their trunks and wait for orders. Maggie retrieves her camera from the car and stands next to me. I take my cue from Agent Hughes and approach John. In a solemn voice, I order, "Lead the way."

Hampered by his shackles, John hobbles along. Abruptly, he stops in his tracks and looks at me. Pointing at his ankles, John pleads, "I can't walk in these woods wearing chains. At this pace, we'll never get where we're going."

I look over my shoulder as the two agents approach. When they get close enough to evaluate the situation, I say, "What do you think?"

They quietly confer. Agreeing to the prisoner's request, Agent Reilly bends down and removes the iron anklets. When he stands upright, the agent removes his gun from its holster. He makes eye contact with John and threatens, "Just give me an excuse."

Free of his chains, the big man walks at a steady pace. He leads us deep into the forest. When we reach a small clearing, John points at two mounds of dirt. The state troopers go into training mode. One man marks the area with crime tape. The other five start digging. As dirt flies through the air, John shouts, "I didn't bury them too deep! I have a bad back and weak knees!"

Undaunted by his remark, the state troopers keep digging. As red clay is lifted and moved, we wait in silence. When human bones are exposed, the officers fall to their knees and dig with their hands. In a short while, the skeletal remains of two victims are unearthed. Maggie snaps the shutter button on her camera and documents the find. In a husky voice, Agent Hughes stares at John and asks, "Who are they?"

Apathetic, John replies, "Lone Wolf and a runaway boy." He sniffs and wipes his nose with his shackled hands before confiding, "He said his name was Steve. That's all I know."

Organizing his recovery team, Agent Hughes shouts out, "Watts and Pearson stay here! The rest of you bring your shovels and come with us!"

Getting my silent cue from Agent Reilly, I look at John and order, "Let's go find Billy."

Our entourage follows the prisoner deeper into

the woods. The underbrush makes the hike difficult but not impassable. We walk about a quarter of a mile before we reach another clearing. The setting is eerily serene. A variety of birdcalls can be heard high in the trees. The water in the nearby stream laps against the shoreline. Overgrown rosebushes surround the mound of earth marked by a granite boulder. Roughly etched in the makeshift headstone are the words, *Here lies Billy Bond, a beautiful young man.* Physically sickened at finding Billy's remains, I glare at John and press, "Are you absolutely certain these are all the graves?"

Showing no signs of remorse, John responds, "Yep, these are all the graves I dug. I can't speak for anybody else."

As soon as I'm convinced John is telling the truth, I sprint over to a tree and vomit. After physically expelling his stench from my system, I rejoin the group. I take Maggie's arm and address Agent Hughes, saying, Our work here is done." Giving him a firm handshake, I state, "Now, I need to inform the mother of the victim before the news gets out. If you haven't any objections, Maggie and I are leaving."

Agent Hughes replies, "I don't blame you for wanting to leave this morbid scene." Shaking my hand, he adds, "Thanks for breaking this case. The bureau had no idea a serial killer was lurking in these mountains. If you hadn't been searching for a missing boy, there's no telling how many more children John would've murdered."

The agent turns and focuses on Maggie. With a

somber expression on his face, he states, "I understand you are the catalyst that spawned this investigation. Thanks for not letting time get in the way of justice."

As Maggie and Agent Hughes talk, Agent Reilly approaches me and inquires, "Where do you go from here."

I answer, "After I inform Betsy of her son's fate, I have some loose ends to wrap up."

Agent Reilly remarks, "It looks like you've gotten emotionally involved in this case?"

I take a moment to think before responding, "It pains me to admit it but I did let my guard down."

Noting the sadness in my eyes, the agent confides, "It's hard to witness crimes against children and remain objective. But, it's essential to remember people like us separate man from beast. The public needs us to do its dirty work. And, we need the public to remind us why we do it." He takes a deep breath and continues, "This is exactly why Ms. Harlow should warn the public of this form of predator."

Maggie hears his words as she approaches. On the verge of tears, she looks at the agent and exclaims, "Thank you, I needed to hear that."

As the two of us turn to head out of the woods, John cries, "Jason, please don't' leave me alone with these men! I'm afraid!"

Fed up with his pathetic act, I whirl around and

expel all the hostility I've suppressed for the past ten days. I scream, "You're afraid! How do you think your victims felt! I don't give a shit about you, you pompous asshole! I played you for a fool because I needed to know where the bodies were buried!" As John hunches down and backs away, I catch my breath and snarl, "Make no mistake! I'm not your friend! Because of me, you're going to be given a lethal injection and die! And, I'll be there watching! I want to be the last thing you see before you go straight to Hell, you sick son of a bitch!"

I turn on my heels and grab Maggie's arm. For a brief moment, she resist as she contemplates making a statement of her own. Then, she decides not to give John the satisfaction. Holding her head high in the air, Maggie whispers, "He is not worth it. Let's get out of here."

Chapter 19

Closure

Maggie and I travel to Asheville with minimal conversation. I'm lost in thought. She's thinking about her issues. Both of us are acutely aware that our lives have been compromised by this case. Neither of us knows how it will influence our future. We check into the Grove Park Inn. Feeling contaminated by John and his morbid graveyard, Maggie and I go straight to our individual rooms. I take a long, hot shower. Afterwards, I dress in casual attire and meet Maggie in the hotel restaurant. After dinner, we call it a night. When the hour grows late, I fall asleep in my own bed.

******

I wake up at six thirty on Wednesday morning, May 21th. I put on sweats and go jogging. When I return to my room, I find Maggie talking on the telephone. She hands me the receiver and whispers, "The ringing woke me. It's Bobby. I'll get dressed while the two of you talk."

After she exits the room, I ask, "What's

happening?"

Bobby responds, "Nothing I can't handle." After a brief pause, he inquires, "What's going on in your neck of the woods?"

I answer, "John confessed to killing eight people, including Billy Bond. Before the media broadcasts the news, I'm going to inform Betsy. Then, I'll speak with the other families." I pause a moment before continuing, "I'll be back in Atlanta late Thursday or Friday morning."

Bobby offers, "Is there anything I can do?"

I give a negative response and hang up the phone. Taking a deep breath, I call and schedule appointments. Satisfied with my itinerary, I shower, shave and dress in casual attire.

Immediately after breakfast, Maggie and I head to the Baptist church. We enter the chapel and spy the preacher standing near the altar. As we approach, Pastor Brown nods his head in recognition. Although he is indifferent to Maggie, it is painfully obvious he considers me obtrusive. Only because of his position in the church does the minister extend us a small degree of civility. I introduce Maggie. Before the preacher has a chance to acknowledge her, I state, "I've come to inform you Deacon John confessed to the campground murders. He also admitted to killing Billy Bond, Lone Wolf and another boy." As the pastor gasps in shock and horror, I continue, "We need to speak privately about financial restitution."

At a loss for words, Pastor Brown leads us into his office. After we sit down, the minister exclaims, "Every member of this congregation will be saddened and appalled by John's heinous actions. I'll never be able to adequately express the deep sympathy we at the church feel for the victims and their families." As Maggie and I stare at the elderly man, beads of perspiration appear on his forehead. Trying to maintain control of the situation, the church official states, "However, it's not the church's obligation to assume financial responsibility for its clerics."

Not the least bit surprised by his attitude and denial of responsibility, I counter, "If the first five murders had been the beginning and end of John's killing spree, I might agree with you; but you and your elders never considered the possibility John might be guilty of murder and continued to sanction his position. Consequently, the facts speak for themselves. This church and its hierarchy are criminally negligent."

Pastor Brown waves his arm in protest. Unable to excuse the church's duplicity, he tries to put me on the defensive. Questioning my motives, he snarls, "Why are you making this church your scapegoat?"

Trying desperately to suppress my rage, I clench my fists. With deliberate control, I reply, "When Billy went missing; this church had a second chance to redeem itself. Again, the hierarchy turned a blind eye and deaf ear to the protests and suspicions of his mother. You and the elders stereotyped her as a poor, dumb illiterate and swept her despair under the doormat of this very building."

Pastor Brown's face turns beet red. He protests, "You can't fault the church for not knowing who to believe?"

With a vengeance, I retaliate, "This is where you're dead wrong! In the first place, there shouldn't be any social activities sponsored by a church where only one adult is present. Secondly, when five boys were slaughtered on a church outing and the chaperone returned with superficial injuries, the church should have demanded to know why he alone managed to escape alive. Third and foremost, this church should have offered moral and financial support to the survivors. And at the very least, the elders should have defrocked John, kicked him out of the building and applauded when he landed on his big, fat ass!"

Pastor Brown refuses to accept my condemnation. He motions for me to quiet down. Frowning at him, I shake my head in disgust. I look him squarely in the eyes and warn, "It would be a heavy cross to bear if this church is involved in a civil lawsuit. I don't think your congregation will appreciate or tolerate the disparaging publicity."

Pastor Brown turns white as a sheet as Maggie and I exit his office. While we walk to our car, Maggie admits, "You never cease to amaze me. I would never have thought of holding the church financially responsible. But, you're absolutely right. No church should allow children to be taken off the property without the supervision of two or more adults." She catches her breath and agrees, "This church is partially responsible for all those deaths."

Frowning, I remark, "I guess you have to settle for whatever justice you can get. After this church digs deep in its pocket, this will be one place where children will be safe from preying monsters."

******

Maggie and I arrive at Betsy's apartment. After one knock, she opens the door. The worried woman focuses on me, waiting for my report. Sensing bad news, she clutches her throat and cries, "You found Billy?"

At a loss for words, I stand and look at Betsy. Reading my mind, she screams in anguish. Maggie reaches for the frail woman and hugs her tightly. Trying to soothe her pain, Maggie whispers, "It was an accident. Deacon John had been making sexual advances toward Billy. Your son wanted no part of it. He tried to get away but he couldn't escape."

Betsy pulls away from Maggie. She looks up at me for answers. Picking up where Maggie left off, I confide, "After the movie, John found Billy and chased him down. When he caught him, your boy fought back. The deacon backhanded him and broke his neck. ... Billy didn't suffer. It was an instant death."

Betsy cries hysterically. While Maggie consoles the weeping woman, I stand and wait for her moment of truth to pass. When she finally stops crying, Betsy collapses on the couch. Maggie sits down beside her. Not knowing what else to do, I take a seat in a nearby chair.

Drying her eyes, Betsy asks, "Will there be a trial?"

Shaking my head, I answer, "Since John confessed, a trial won't be necessary. There will be a hearing followed by sentencing."

In a shallow voice, Betsy inquires, "Will he get the death penalty?"

I reply, "I believe he will. He murdered eight people. He sexually molested at least one of them. I don't think any judge in the country would let him escape the death penalty."

Maggie and I stay with Betsy for nearly an hour. When the time is right, I advise her of my ultimatum to the church. I ask her to keep me informed. Shortly afterwards, Maggie and I make our excuses and leave Betsy to grieve for her son.

******

Maggie and I arrive at the Campbell residence a few minutes early. Answering my knock, Lilly swings the door open. She motions for us to come inside. She smiles at me and I peck her on the cheek. Blushing, Lilly gestures for us to sit down on the sofa. She takes a seat in the rocking chair positioned near the window.

I face Lilly and begin, "Deacon John confessed

to murdering Rusty and the other four boys." As tears roll down her cheeks, I continue, "He's in the custody of the State Bureau of Investigation. Since he admitted to the murders, a trial won't be necessary. From here on out, it's just a matter of formality. He will plead 'Guilty' at his arraignment. Then, a court date will be set for sentencing."

Dabbing at her eyes, Lilly asks, "What about Betsy's boy, Billy?"

I answer, "John admitted to killing Billy and two other people. He molested a lot of boys over the years; but he swears he only killed the ones who threatened to expose him."

Curious, Lilly inquires, "Why did he confess after all these years?"

I shrug my shoulders. Maggie answers for me, saying, "We're not sure." She pauses for a moment and then elaborates, "We found a letter written by Jason, providing the details as to how John murdered Rusty, Charlie and Steve. The handwritten note justified a warrant. After he was in custody, John confessed."

Not satisfied with her explanation, Lilly looks at me and pries, "Who got him to confess?" Before I can answer her question, she guesses, "It was you, wasn't it?"

I nod my head to confirm her suspicion. Glancing at Maggie, Lilly points at me and exclaims, "Just look at those eyes! Not even Satan himself could look into those eyes and lie!" Neither of us comments. Making her point, she goes on, "When you gaze into those steel blue eyes, it's like looking into a mirror. You can't life to yourself ; so, you speak the truth."

Flattered but slightly embarrassed, I change the subject and advise, "Lilly, I've spoken to Pastor Brown. The church should offer you a financial settlement within the next several weeks." As her anger surfaces, Lilly's face reddens. Before she can protest, I counter, "Don't consider it payment for your son's life. It is retribution. By offering compensation, the church won't make the same mistake twice. I need you to accept the money to protect other innocent children."

Maggie and I stay with Lilly long enough for her to calm her nerves. When we feel relatively sure she has come to terms with the dreadful news, Maggie and I rise to leave. Feeling the need to further persuade her to follow through on the church's settlement, I suggest, "Rusty would want you to have the money and improve your living conditions. Do it for him."

Taking my argument to heart, Lilly agrees, "I'll take the money if you think I should. And, for that reason alone."

Pleased with her decision, I hand Lilly my business card and state, "If you don't receive an offer by June 14th, call me."

Lilly takes the card and places it on the table by her telephone. She hugs Maggie and me. As she holds me close, Lilly whispers in my ear, "Thank you so much for caring about my son. I can never tell you how much it means to me."

After we walk outside, Lilly closes the door. Tears flood her eyes. She says a silent prayer, thanking God for bringing us to her door.

******

En route to the city, tears run down Maggie's face. She sobs, "The past two weeks have been an emotional roller coaster. I've met some wonderful people, you included. But the vile influence of John has tainted this experience."

I look over at Maggie and say, "It takes opposites to balance the world. Where there is good, there is evil. It's Universal Law."

Maggie wipes her eyes with a Kleenex and asks, "How can you deal with criminals on a constant basis and keep a positive attitude?"

Trying to make light of my chosen profession, I quip, "Because I'm positively driven to catch bad guys."

Maggie laughs and retorts, "There's no way to get the best of you. I guess I have to accept your quest to rid the world of crime."

I respond, "And I must accept your calling to report the good, the bad and the evil."

******

Maggie and I kill a few hours window-shopping.

We dine at a local restaurant and spend another hour touring the city streets. At seven forty-five, I steer the car in the direction of the Simmons' home.

Jennifer answers the door and leads us into the living room. Maggie and I sit on the couch. Jennifer plops down on the loveseat. Rob sits in the same chair he occupied during our previous visit. I glance at Rob. Then, I focus on Jennifer and say, "I've come to inform you Deacon John confessed to murdering Jimmy and the other four boys on the camping trip." She clutches her throat and lets out a cry. Without waiting for her to comment, I go on, "He also admitted to killing three other people: Billy Bond, Lone Wolf and a runaway boy."

Dumbfounded, Jennifer gasps, "Are you sure you're talking about our Deacon John?"

I answer, "I'm positive. John has been arrested for eight counts of murder. He's in the custody of the State Bureau of Investigation."

Stunned, Jennifer looks at Maggie and questions, "How could a man of God commit murder?"

Maggie responds, "He's a very sick man. Your son was simply in the wrong place at the wrong time."

In shock, Jennifer sobs, "Why?"

I explain, "John is a pedophile. He preys on young boys." Noting the concern on her face, I quickly add, "Jimmy wasn't molested. Rusty Campbell was. Rusty confronted the deacon at the campground. John went into a rage and killed him. The other boys heard Rusty's accusation and witnessed his murder. John killed them to keep his secret and escape prosecution."

Still in shock, Jennifer gasps, "What about Lone Wolf?"

I answer, "Lone Wolf caught John molesting a young boy. John killed both of them to keep people from finding out he was a pedophile ... and murderer."

Suddenly and unexpectedly, Rob blurts out, "Tom Frazier told me that son-of-a-bitch did it! He never believed John's story! All the while I defended the bastard!" The frail man sobs, "I cursed Tom for implying a church leader could be capable of murder! If I'd only listened to Tom, that monster would've been in jail years ago!"

Stunned by his outburst, the three of us stare at Rob. Still reeling from the shock of hearing the horrible truth, Jennifer looks at me and asks, "Why did it take so long to expose the deacon?"

Offering her thoughts, Maggie speculates, "Everybody, including the local police, assumed John was a victim. There really wasn't any reason to doubt his story." She elaborates, "Both of you believed in the church and its clerics. Tom was literally the only member of this community who suspected John of foul play."

Rob and Jennifer sit in silence, consumed in utter despair. Maggie reaches out by saying, "Please don't become John's victims. Jimmy wouldn't want that. He'd want you to warn other parents about the consequences of blind faith."

Rob asks, "How can I warn other parents?"

I answer, "By telling your story."

Frustrated, Rob argues, "How? I'm not a public figure. I'm just an ordinary man."

Maggie exclaims, "Remember me! I'm a reporter! I plan to write a book about the murders. It would be most helpful if I could include your story."

Crying, Rob gasps, "I'll do anything humanly possible to prevent this kind of tragedy from happening to another family."

Relieved, Maggie advises, "After the hearing and sentencing, I'll return to Asheville and record your account."

Wanting to give Rob a sense of purpose, I add, "The world needs Christian people like you to sound the alarm."

I take a moment to think, *I should tell Rob and Jennifer about the church settlement but Jennifer would be appalled at the thought of monetary gain as a result of her son's murder.* Listening to my inner voice, I decide not to mention this detail. I'm confident the two of them are capable of making a decision as to whether or not to accept an offer at the appropriate time.

As Maggie and I prepare to leave, Jennifer takes my hand and apologizes, "I'm sorry I was so pious when you first came to our home. I truly believed John was a devout Christian, incapable of violence, much less murder. I was a sanctimonious hypocrite. I can't find the proper words to excuse my behavior."

Looking at Jimmy' mother, I respond, "Everyone reacts to tragedy in different ways. Your false image of John kept you sane. Denial kept Rob in a state of despondency. Tom's inability to expose John broke his heart and put him in an early grave." I pause and then continue, "It really doesn't matter how one deals with tragedy. What matters is the truth. The truth is a necessary prelude to closure."

Maggie and I leave the Simmons' home and head back to our motel. En route, I heave a sigh of relief and admit, "My work is done here. I'm ready to go home."

Smiling at me, Maggie confides, "You gave closure to all those families. Now, they can heal." She sighs and continues, "No one could ask for more."

Epilogue

Today is Saturday, August 15, 2010. I'm en route to the George C. Randall building in Raleigh, North Carolina. The execution of John Wesley Powers is scheduled to take place at midnight. My life has changed radically since I crossed his path seven years ago. As I drive, I reminisce:

I returned to Atlanta and my work. For more than six months, Maggie and I avoided each other. She needed time to grieve for Jason. I wanted to separate myself from the case. On New Year's Eve, Maggie and I showed up at the same party. I was with another woman. She was with another man. We left the party together. From that moment on, Maggie and I have been together. We made it official by getting married in June, 2005. We are the proud parents of a boy and girl. Todd's four and Courtney is two. Jay graduated from Oglethorpe College and has joined the state attorney's office in the greater Atlanta area. Aunt Ruth visits on occasion. Bobby is still my partner and our agency is thriving.

Maggie has traveled back and forth between Atlanta and Raleigh on a regular basis. She has interviewed John more times than she'd like to admit. She keeps in touch with the families of the victims. Maggie has documented their personal interaction with the deacon before and after he turned their lives into Hell on Earth. The execution of John Wesley Powers will be the final chapter of her upcoming novel, BLIND FAITH.

As I exit the interstate and head toward the state prison, I'm brought back to the present. I reach the criminal facility and have to dodge the right-to-life advocates to park in the designated area. I get out of my car and follow the signs, guiding me to the proper entrance. After flashing my credentials to the prison guards, I'm ushered inside the building and directed to the elevator. I get on and ride down to the basement. I step out and walk down the narrow corridor to the viewing area. Nodding at the news reporters gathered in the hallway, I reach the door, pull it open and walk inside.

I enter the dimly lit room and wait for my eyes to adjust to the light. When my vision focuses, I spot Jennifer and Rob Simmons sitting on the back row. Jennifer looks the same as she did when I met her; but there is a dramatic improvement in Rob's appearance. He looks fifty pounds heavier and has color in his cheeks. The couple recognizes me and waves. I nod my head, smile and continue to scan the room.

My attention is drawn to Lilly Campbell and Betsy Bond. They are sitting together on the second row. Both women appear solemn but not dismayed. The look of determination of their faces reveals their need to witness the event and close the saddest chapter in their lives. Seeing me, both women smile and nod their heads. I return the friendly gesture.

I don't see Maggie. Her absence bothers me. Concerned, I glance at my watch. Instantaneously, the exterior door opens. The flashbulb of a camera blinds me for a second. When my vision returns to normal, I see Maggie in the company of an older woman. Maggie approaches me and whispers, "Carolyn's plane was late. I couldn't come without her." She catches her breath and continues, "She deserves to witness the end of her nightmare."

I smile at the attractive older woman as she sits down beside Maggie on the front row. I'm distracted when the curtains open and expose the execution area. Suddenly, I'm reminded of my reason for being in this musty, dark and claustrophobic space. With his wrists and ankles secured with lined restraints and covered by a sheet, John lays on a gurney. He watches as the trained personnel enter the area and connect the cardiac monitor, injection devices and stethoscope to the appropriate leads. He listens as the warden informs the audience the execution is about to begin. Finishing his statement, the prison official offers the dead man walking an opportunity to speak and clear his conscience. John declines the offer. The warden disappears back into the chamber.

An eerie silence pervades the small space. I watch as John searches for a familiar face among the viewers. When he spots me in the audience, John focuses on me. I stand unflinching under the most horrible of circumstances. The old man grins and winks at me. Our eyes lock. John's smile fades as the lethal injection enters his bloodstream. His body reacts to the dosage and twitches until his stare goes blank. Everyone in the room has a sickly solemn look on their face, silently watching the EKG monitor. The flat line appears and sounds. The warden checks the prisoner's vital signs before pronouncing John Wesley Powers dead.

During the deathwatch, I raise my eyes and see Carolyn's reflection in the glass. As I stare at her, I watch her matronly image transform into a beautiful young woman. In my head, I hear her sing, "I'm getting married in the morning. Ding, dong! the bells are gonna chime ... Hail and salute me. Then haul off and boot me ... And get me to the church, Get me to the church ... For Gawd's sake, get me to the church on time!"

As I stand spellbound by her vision, Carolyn looks at the mirror reflection of me. She gasps as my adult features transform into the face of young Jason. She hears me, urging, "Dad, can't you drive a little faster?" In her mind, she sees me mouth the words, "I love you, Mom."

Our moment of truth passes in the blink of an eye.

The End

www.ingramcontent.com/pod-product-compliance
Lightning Source LLC
Chambersburg PA
CBHW050924120626
46552CB00001B/25